ALL MY FRIENDS

Marie NDiaye
Translated by Jordan Stump

Two Lines Press

Tous Mes Amis by Marie NDiaye
© 2004 by Les Éditions de Minuit
7, Rue Bernard-Palissy 75006 Paris
Translation © 2013 by Jordan Stump
All rights reserved.

Published by Two Lines Press
582 Market Street, Suite 700, San Francisco, CA 94104
www.twolinespress.com

ISBN 978-1-931883-23-8

Library of Congress Control Number: 2012949424

Design by Ragina Johnson
Cover Design by Gabriele Wilson
Cover Photo by Penny Klepuszewska/Gallery Stock

Printed in the United States of America

ART WORKS.
arts.gov

amazon.com

This project is supported in part by an award from the National Endowment for the
Arts and a grant from Amazon.com.
Cet ouvrage a bénéficié du soutien des Programmes d'aide à la publication
de l'Institut Français.
This work, published as part of a program of aid for publication, received support
from the Institut Français.

Contents

ALL MY FRIENDS

The next time I see Werner, once all this is over, a nervous snicker will be his only greeting. He'll back a few steps away, cautious and, for once, unsure of himself.

I ask Séverine to tell me about her husband, which she does, at first sullenly and reluctantly, and then, seeing me so curious, curtly and parsimoniously.

Here I chide myself for letting my eagerness show. Take it one step at a time with your maid Séverine, I say to myself, she can read you like your own mother.

But Séverine is a full fifteen years my junior, so why all this interest in Séverine's husband, obscure young man that he surely is, just as she is a commonplace charming young woman I pay to come to my house every day and do the tasks I find tedious?

Be patient, be careful with Séverine, I admonish myself, and slink through the tallest grass, and always stop short of your mark.

Because I've sensed from the start that this job does not

mean so much to her that she'd hesitate to walk out on me should something displease her, for example my inquisitorial manner, and since I often feel uncomfortable and contrite to see Séverine doing some chore I could easily deal with, I accuse myself of attempting to abuse her to the fullest by thrusting these honeyed questions on her every time she looks up, for I'm quite aware that she can scarcely have the presence of mind to weigh her words, or hold her tongue, or change the subject when I confront her so unexpectedly that she jumps on her way out of the bathroom, still flushed and tousled from bending into my deep tub.

Little by little, inside me, a knowledge of Séverine's husband is taking shape. I know the rudiments: he works in the post office, like Séverine he's thirty years old, his hair and eyes are such-and-such a color, and so forth.

It takes me a good while to work up my courage and ask her if…

I come serenely to Séverine, give her my caring, courtly smile, part my lips, but certain forthright words stay stuck in my throat. Séverine looks at me with her narrow golden eyes, surprised, then shrugs and goes on her way, tactfully sidestepping me.

I position myself in the hall, arms outstretched to block the way. Séverine comes out of my bedroom, empty-handed, as if she has nothing to do. In a loud, husky voice I blurt out:

"Do you love your husband, Séverine?"

For those are the words I couldn't bring myself to speak before.

Séverine's eyebrows come together, knit in anger. She

stares into my eyes. But I hold her gaze, and after an awkward moment she finds herself forced to look away.

"Do you, Séverine, love your husband?"

My pleasure at saying this makes my voice slightly shrill.

Séverine slowly comes toward me. Her arms swing back and forth, her chin is raised, lips clenched in indignation. I've never seen my maid Séverine so angry with me. Could it be that she doesn't dare answer? She keeps coming till she's standing against me, her very round breasts touching my chest, compressing it slightly with their heavy, unyielding weight. Séverine outstrips me, not by her height, which is close to my own, but by the density of her muscles, the solidity of her flesh. Again I cry out, enchanted by the words:

"Séverine, do you love your husband?"

Séverine's gleaming eyes darken, and between two lashes a tiny teardrop appears, quivers, then falls onto my shoulder. But, although I believe I can feel a caustic substance eating into my skin at that spot, I see that Séverine is still enraged and surprised.

Séverine answers that, for one thing, she does love her husband (Oh, she loves him, I tell myself, downhearted), and for another, she's leaving me here and now, as I had absolutely no right to ask such a question.

My maid Séverine was a student of mine in junior high, and I chose Séverine to come work in my house precisely because I recalled how she tormented me with her absurd, arrogant, self-absorbed behavior as a beautiful teenager, lazy and bold, one among many, though none terrorized me like this Séverine, with her bird-of-prey stare—direct, yellow, unwavering.

Séverine clearly took great joy in fixing me with her cold, piercing gaze from the back of the classroom, eyeing me with relentless disdain as I stood exposed and frantic at the blackboard, until, exasperated, afraid, I let out an acerbic laugh and threatened her with sanctions if she didn't look down at her workbook at once.

Séverine never obeyed. She'd raise one mocking eyebrow, still observing me. Sometimes, in a murmur, she answered: "But I'm not looking at you," which set off such an explosion of hilarity inside me that I had to hurry out of the room, gasping, wretched, while she stayed just where she was, the imperturbable Séverine, perhaps even, who knows, taking my place at the board until, many long minutes later, my laughter and turmoil finally abated.

Now I have to beg Séverine's forgiveness, and convince her to come back.

Before I do, I stop by the post office. I've had dealings with that round-cheeked boy before, perfectly pleasant and sharp, I remember his little wire-rimmed glasses and thick black hair, but I had no idea he was Séverine's husband.

Now I know. Emboldened by this vital information, I hold my head high, and at that very moment some sort of mirror mysteriously hanging in the very atmosphere of that cramped post office reflects a new image of me: slender, well-dressed, distinguished profile, straight nose. Flustered but secretly pleased, I say to myself: still a fine figure of a man.

I gently rest my forehead on the pane of glass that separates me from Séverine's husband.

How troubling it is to remember the loathing I felt for my student Séverine, and to think of the affection I feel for my maid Séverine. Are they even the same girl? I sometimes wonder.

The very young Séverine mistreated me horribly, despite all the pains I took with her, all the efforts I devoted to seeing her succeed, all the special warmth I might have seemed to feel for her, though that's not how it was. It was my fear of Séverine that made me seek out her favor, her blessing. But there was no indulgence, no pity, not even coherence. How many times, in this very house that Séverine now halfheartedly cleans, saving her strength for activities unknown to me, how many times did I await her in vain, to give her, free of charge, the supplementary lessons she so sorely needed, and how many times did I drift off to sleep as I waited, beside the window where I'd been watching for her, and such a bitter, lost sleep it was? One morning I found the courage to scold her for failing to show, and in the soft, slightly breathless voice Séverine liked to use with me, she answered: "But I did come," and I shuddered to think that, if she truly had crept into the house then she'd seen me in the anguish of my sad sleep, towering over me, perhaps tempted to… to what? This Séverine, who knew nothing of anxiety, who was all reproval, pitiless judgment, disdain—this Séverine, I said to myself, oh, what Séverine? In my vulnerable state, in my solitude, what might this girl have done to me? I had no idea.

I still hoped to teach Séverine all I knew, but, intelligent though she was, Séverine shoved my lessons aside, with the discreet but unambiguous gesture that pushes away a dish of questionable food. My idea is that Séverine had chosen to sacrifice her education simply so as to receive nothing from me, and when a rational voice, rising from some spot in my empty house, assures me that this scarcely seems likely, I remain convinced all the same, however powerless to prove it.

Nothing I said was to stay inside her. I was a passionate man, and I was a passionate teacher, and that girl with the gaze of stone, that Séverine, disapproved of such passion. I had acquired a certain mastery in the art of beguiling my students. In the junior high school, in the high school, my enviable popularity had long been a matter of record. And that was precisely what Séverine condemned, never saying so outright, and so she coldly resisted it, preventing any intrusion of my knowledge into her clear, empty mind, sparing herself any commingling with me.

I tried to force her. I put my arm around her broad shoulders to help with an exercise she refused to let her mind even touch. In my turn, I stared into her yellow eyes, smiling deliberately, insistently, and I snapped my fingers before her closed face as if to invite her to dance, and I murmured:

"Séverine, I'm going to lend you some books, and you'll read them, and then you'll tell me about them."

But not one of the many books lent to Séverine was ever returned, was ever the subject of any discussion, ever revealed that Séverine's character had been affected by it, or her hatred for me reduced.

"Tell Séverine I'm sorry for being so curious," I whisper to Séverine's husband through the glass at the post-office counter.

Studying him at such close range, I'm disturbed and surprised to see Séverine's husband for what he is, and unhappy with that girl for concealing what matters most about him.

He asks me what business I'd like to transact.

"None," I say, a little flustered.

And then, to that attentive young man:

"Don't you recognize me?"

I feel very alone. The glance I then give Séverine's husband must be pleading or anxious, for in a low, kindly voice he replies that Séverine has already decided to keep working for me. I go on my way, listless, smelling the scornful workings of a conspiracy, a condescension, in the air of the street. And what my nose senses is confirmed by what I see on the opposite sidewalk, all aglow with a heart-wrenching gaiety: my wife and children, all three having long since made up their minds not to speak to me again, walking with long, lively strides toward the house that they live in without me.

Scurrying to keep up, I call out, first to my two sons and then to my wife.

"How are you doing?" I shout, forcing myself to sound cheerful, lighthearted.

They briefly turn their irritated gaze on me, three pairs of dark eyes, all identical and similarly hostile, then hurry off toward the avenue that I theoretically don't even have the right to walk down.

Later, once Werner has come back to town, I'll confide in him on the subject of my wife and children, and though Werner is far younger than I am he will lighten my burden, saying, for example, in his cultivated voice, "Are you supposed to spend your whole life making amends? Your whole life being punished?" And his fervid serenity, and the unshakable certitude of his pragmatism, will bit by bit lead me to find it unfair, contrary to what I once thought, that I should think myself condemned to spend my entire life expiating the mistakes or the crimes I committed (yes, it's true—unless that's not exactly what they were?) against my own family. Ensconced in my best armchair, his handsome, disquieting face making me forget the disquiet that my house's desolate, whispering depths inspire in me every night (for my house doesn't like me), Werner will force me to regain some of the self-respect, poise, and excellence I'd been fleetingly shown by the broad mirror that hung in the air when I stopped by the post office.

My wife and children made an ally of my house, where they once lived, where they no longer live. My house misses my children's games and my wife's wrenching cries, my house jealously envies that other house they now live in, unknown and modern. And on that point, far from laughing at my terrors and precautions, Werner will murmur, with a kindheartedness that brings tears to my eyes: "Don't forget, you're the master of your house." It sounds so innocent when Werner says it. I must neither fear my house nor beg it to forgive me for being alone.

I am the master of my house.

Séverine comes by while I'm still away at school. Surprised to see the lights on in my house, I stand for a moment in the rain, my face raised toward the living room window, and I see Séverine pacing slowly back and forth, moving her lips, sometimes smiling into the little phone she keeps clasped to her ear.

With some sheepishness I remember a tiny gold phone I once confiscated from Séverine, thinking I'd heard it ring during class. I want to bring that incident up with Séverine. But Séverine's never shown any sign of remembering me as her ex-teacher. Never has Séverine seemed to recall that connection between us, fifteen years back, and whenever, irritated, I've found myself on the verge of spitting out: "What did you do with those books I lent you, Séverine?" I've always kept quiet, lips pressed together, for fear I might see Séverine narrow her wary eyes in incomprehension, and so realize she's fulfilled her pledge to allow no germ of my being into her person, since she has deeply and utterly forgotten me.

I rush into the house, excited and relieved. I say to Séverine:

"I'm so happy to see you again, Séverine."

And then my joy gets the better of me, and I add:

"That telephone of yours, Séverine, is it the one I took away from you, then gave back at the very end of the year?"

Séverine doesn't answer. She carefully rehooks the telephone to her belt, she gathers up her long chestnut hair and fixes it behind her neck. Séverine pirouettes on her sleek athletic shoes, colored a victorious silver. She walks away, muttering that she's going up to do my room.

I find this extremely unpleasant. I feel ashamed and resentful. Toward Séverine's back, toward her broad, unfriendly, puritanical back, I snap:

"Why didn't you tell me your husband's an Arab? Why didn't you tell me I know him, Séverine? Why did you want to keep those two things from me, Séverine?"

Séverine freezes in the entryway, at the foot of the big black staircase that leads up to my room, as well as my children's old rooms, still untouched, still crammed with their baby clothes and their toys, though my children are now in their teens, as if they'd fled with such haste that there was no time to take anything with them. Séverine looks back. In a self-possessed voice, she tells me I'm clearly mistaken, because there's no way I could have met her husband before.

"No, you're the one who's mistaken, Séverine."

I speak calmly. I have no wish to gloat, even if I'm right. My feelings are hurt. Like my house, Séverine doesn't like me. Nevertheless, I speak calmly.

"Your husband was my student, Séverine. He was in your class, and he was the only Arab in that class, so I remember him well. Which means that you met him in high school, Séverine."

Séverine snickers. Her discomfort and melancholy undulate heavily between us.

She starts up the black staircase, empty-handed, as if, rather than clean, she was planning to lie down for a nap in my room. Then, reaching the top, she leans over the banister, and I think I she's falling, throwing herself over. But she merely repeats that there's no way I could have met her

husband before, and I'm obviously confusing him with someone else. And I think I see her detach something from her
neck and drop it my way, and I think I can feel a youthful
human skin falling over my feet, a skin heavy with rancor
and bitterness.

I don't remember Séverine's husband's name, because it's a
complicated name, which I found difficult to hold in my
memory even then. But I do recall Werner's name, includ-
ing his real first name. And when, later, I enter Werner's
luxurious house, when I timidly take my place in one of
his armchairs, upholstered in a pale green leather so fine-
grained it will make me think of Séverine's neck and arms,
I'll squint slightly to fend off the dazzling light from the
bare picture windows and observe that the sun always shines
with extraordinary brightness in Werner's garden, and
that this excess seems to have established itself as a banal,
inevitable amenity of the house, like the many bathrooms
and the three communicating salons, and then, gently bask-
ing in the warmth pouring through the panes, eyes half-
closed, as happy as if it were one of my sons hosting me, I
will ask Werner:

"Why did you change your first name, Werner?"

"Because it's the same as yours," Werner will answer, in
the crisp, precise, slightly proud voice of the excellent student
who was once mine, and which aroused in me, at the time, a
certain antipathy.

Vaguely hurt, I'll say nothing, wondering why this young
man, whom I'd taught with no small devotion, who was fond

of me, who might even, discreetly, have admired me, should, having attained a loftier standing than mine, find it appropriate to turn up his nose at what made him, what propelled him to the place he now occupies, to the lavish and ridiculous house I'll be so pleased to visit and sit down in, for that house will treat me fairly and lovingly.

Unmoved by my lot, Werner will add, coolly:

"Because it's the same as yours, and Séverine used to hate that."

He will smile his disturbing little smile, disillusioned and sorrowful but devoid of compassion, thoughtfulness, or curiosity. All around me, Werner's house will offer its protection. The spirit of the house will disengage from Werner to come closer to me, understanding that for Werner the house is only a tool, and not the object of an affection that I myself wholeheartedly feel for it, asking nothing in return.

And Werner will offer me a drink, and I'll jump. I'll even begin to tremble a little. Raising one arm as if he's threatened to strike me, I'll say:

"No, no. No alcohol, never again."

And oh, his distant smile, his detachment as he pours himself a glass of something or other, wanting to know nothing more about me!

And why the other one, then, Séverine's husband? Why a husband for Séverine? How did that ever happen?

Séverine's husband, the only Arab in the class, enjoyed a special protection and benevolence on my part, mediocre student though he was, and is it not absurd, is it not a sign of my blindness that I treated him with more care than I did Werner, who did my teaching proud, who played a palpable role in the establishment of my renown, but whom I didn't like, for whom I had no regard, whom I never favored, despite his superior grades and his personal charm? Was I not misguided? Oh yes, I was misguided, misguided, misguided. For Werner's parents were notoriously bourgeois, and on those simple grounds I allowed myself, with a perfectly clear conscience, to feel a disdain tinged with aversion for the young man who was not then named Werner, never particularly troubling to hide it from Werner, very likely assuming that having two medical-specialist parents is reason enough for anyone to expect no consideration or friendship from others.

I will come to Werner's house, I'll relax gratefully in one of his armchairs, upholstered in something very like silken female skin, though light green. But even as I enfold Werner in a thankful, expectant gaze, I will find a remorse, a sense of my own duplicity and foolishness, a vague fear tarnishing my pleasure and quietude in spite of me. Because I used to curse Werner, for living in the town center's finest neighborhood. And his elegant little leather jackets, his brand-name jeans, his smart haircut, his countless pairs of athletic shoes, I hated all that with a slightly painful relish, remembering some boy or other, very like Werner, who'd tormented me for my pathetic appearance when I was fifteen.

And yet I will now find myself in the thrall of Werner's house, driven from my own by an indecipherable tyranny.

And yet I will now find myself in the thrall of Werner himself, not so much of that young man who was once my student, not so much of him as of all that comes with him: my earlier misjudgment, his friendly house, his single-minded longing for Séverine, his comfort, his wealth. Before everything I once resisted, fighting off the temptation to envy him or find him impressive, I will lay down my arms. And I'll watch Werner gracefully come and go, I'll hear him offer me comforting words, offhanded, with no real friendship, simply because he has in his house a frightened and lonely man and has learned that one has a duty to say comforting words to those in my situation. I'll tell him of the treachery of my house, my wife, and my sons, who, on abandoning me, lost all consciousness of my existence. I will vehemently refuse any alcohol. Nevertheless, I will never tell him how I once hated him, and when that memory comes back, with Werner there before me, I will blush in humiliation, unable to stop it, a simple-minded smile on my lips. I will be so unhappy that it makes Werner uncomfortable, Werner who enjoys such a mastery over his emotions.

I ask Séverine if she remembers that boy who now calls himself Werner. Standing before the big mirror in the entryway, Séverine stretches, fists clenched and raised high above her head, eyes half shut. I glimpse the creamy skin around her very deep navel, revealed by the pink sweater pulled up almost to the base of her breasts by Séverine's pose.

"This Werner was in your high-school class, Séverine, and his real name is the same as my own. He went off to study and work in Paris, and now he's back with us, and, Séverine, you're the reason he's here."

I speak in a murmur, as overcome with emotion as if I were asking for Séverine's hand.

"I taught you all, and that boy was the most brilliant student I've ever had, Séverine," I add, with the vanity of a father.

Séverine eyes me coldly in the mirror. Slowly she lowers her arms, virtuous and assured, and I know that, perfectly confident in her own austerity, she would be no less unembarrassed or brusque had I actually seen her breasts.

Séverine did no work that morning. She drifted through the house, opening and closing the doors, tapping the furniture with a bent index finger, a discreetly critical expression on her dispassionate face. She seemed to be playing at inspecting my house like a potential buyer, but, roleplay being foreign to Séverine's nature, I thought in a sort of outraged dismay that Séverine might actually covet my house. I could see that she felt no fear of the place. The empty upper-floor rooms greeted her pleasantly. I took note of all that with some gloom.

Séverine then answers my question: yes, she remembers Werner. To my great surprise, she adds that she once dated Werner, then left him for another boy, now her husband, and today they're all thirty years old, meaning that these adventures date back to a distant, apocryphal, and even unlikely past.

"Ah yes, your husband, Séverine," I say peevishly. "Do you believe your husband will ever do better than a job at the post office counter, Séverine? He was not a good student, not a good student at all. I believe, Séverine, that the past deserves our trust and respect, and I believe you have no right to consider the Werner question closed."

But I stop there, shocked at myself, and fall into torrents of apologies, already cringing at what I see gleaming in Séverine's bronze-colored eye: a pure, sovereign anger whose legitimacy enrages me.

I remember the pitiful grades that once disgraced Séverine's work, like that of the boy who became her husband, I remember the peculiarity they shared, a total absence of the ugliness and indignity that reveals itself now and then on the brows of all backward students. Indeed, as I often vaguely reflected, did not the blot of their incompetence, displayed before the whole class, sometimes land on me, me, unjustly and incomprehensibly? As if the dishonor of a grotesquely bad grade lay with me, I who had written that grade with my own hand, and not with them, they who merely accepted it, without really accepting it, arrogant as ever. They think they're too fine for all this, I often seethed, they want to play artist, and they feel only disdain for the teacher who sweats for them, stammering in his excitement and his yearning to please.

Séverine unhooks her telephone from her belt. She tosses her head to shake back the bounteous curls that cover her ear, which is tiny and pierced with three holes, always left unadorned. I notice the fine lines delicately incised at the corners of her eyes. A gentle stupor keeps my gaze glued to Séverine's cheek, her straight mouth, her small nose, and I ask myself: is this the same person?, knowing perfectly well, but could my ex-student Séverine really have gone from sixteen to thirty without those many passing years in any way altering my own existence, without my having done anything other than languish and age? No, I tell myself slowly, it's out of the question, out of the question.

Lulled by Séverine's murmurs into the phone, I realize with a start that she's talking to my wife. She calls her "Madame," then the name that belonged to my wife when I met her. Séverine turns off the phone. She looks into my helpless eyes, her gaze hard, intractable, authoritarian, icy with morality and truth. Sharply, Séverine tells me she knows of the harm I did to my family, my wife having told her on learning that Séverine was in my employ. Séverine knows all there is to know about that, she assures me. Séverine glowers at me, almost fanatically sure of herself and her unassailability.

"Can I not be pardoned someday, Séverine?" I say, wretched, blindsided. "Can I never be absolved, Séverine? Someday?"

Séverine then tells me that what I did can't be forgiven, and, in the incorruptibility of her rigor, it's as if she herself were the victim of my misdeeds.

"Why did you marry that boy, Séverine?" I ask. "Werner's the one you…"

But Séverine cuts me off with a sharp bark. Séverine tells me I must never speak of her husband again, and that, should I dare do so, she will lay out all my misdeeds, all the awful things I've said, exhaustively catalogued for her by my wife.

Confounded, I mumble:

"What you don't know, Séverine, is that I couldn't always

control what I said or did, that there were, Séverine, circumstances which..."

None of that interests her, Séverine tells me. And as the fire in her yellow eyes dims I see that she means it, that the reasons for my behavior bore her in advance, that it wearies her even to consider the possibility that there might have been reasons and moments.

"Do you remember that my wife was your teacher, Séverine?" I ask her.

Séverine tells me she does.

"Then why won't you remember that I was your teacher as well?" I explode.

Patiently, Séverine explains that my wife was an excellent teacher, and that to this day she remembers her, my wife as a teacher, with great fondness.

"Well, that hardly seems fair, Séverine."

I snicker, but I'm devastated.

My wife and I never talked about Séverine when she was our student, my wife because in her class Séverine was a passive and unexceptional pupil, me because Séverine persecuted me in silence, disrupting my lessons with her poisonous enmity. And now that my wife has left me, abandoned me to myself and my house's little machinations, now she's won Séverine to her side, now she's staked out a marvelous, unparalleled place in Séverine's memory, when the fact is I know that my wife is a cynical and irascible teacher.

To what end should she seek to make Séverine her ally, fifteen years after the fact? And forever distance Séverine from me, Séverine and her innocent, fierce inflexibility?

My wife's prying spirit scuttles through my house, hungry for vengeance. At school, my reputation is secure and longstanding, whereas my wife's teaching and personality enjoy no special renown, despite all her efforts, when she left me, to gain our little clan of envious colleagues' sympathy and approval. To be sure, now my wife's gaze never meets mine in the hallways. To be sure, I sometimes come nose to nose with one of my sons on the playground, and how painful it is to see his eyes, having lighted on me by accident, suddenly fill with a sort of still water before he turns on his heel and flees, his gait slightly stiff, horrified.

"Is your father a swine?" I sometimes cry after him.

And to be sure, I can no longer pretend not to see that the shop teacher whose mailbox adjoins mine in our break room now lives with my wife and my children in their new house, a rival to my own. But…

"Does your father stink so horribly, that you have to run?" I sometimes cry after my son.

My voice breaks. I no longer know my children, brought up to feel only contempt for their father. The shop teacher looks after my children alongside my wife, he raises and loves them as if they were his own, and, when I see my children's radiant faces and, from snatches of conversation made out here and there, learn of their excellent grades, I must admit that he's raising them in the best possible way, and when we bump elbows he unfailingly treats me with the same polite sympathy, cool and impeccable. To be sure, what better can I expect? To whom can I complain? I myself put on a cheerful, good-hearted air with everyone around me. To whom can I complain, why complain? I simply find it unjust, when my wife never seemed to trouble herself over Séverine's future as I did, that she should now use the fact that she's of the same sex as Séverine, and lives a happier life than my own, to prevent Séverine from looking on me with solicitude, compassion, and neutrality. Deep inside me, in a place I never go, where I would find it slightly ignoble to want to go, an urge for revolt is swelling, and it shortens my breath and sharpens my voice.

Werner clearly recalls the year when my wife was his teacher, and recalls, too, that at the time Séverine confessed to her great pleasure on heading into my wife's classroom.

"I find that very surprising," I say, annoyed.

Settled into one of Werner's armchairs, legs crossed, I note with a sort of panic that boredom and impatience dull Werner's fine, glowing face with this mention of my wife's teaching. I know that Werner came to me only because Séverine works in my house. But I'd like to think that my incongruous presence in his own house, the house of a flourishing adult, reminds him with some nostalgia of a time when I nourished his keen mind, when it was I who paced back and forth before his raised, attentive eyes, my size, my voice, and my power all working for me at once. Werner has moved into the suburbs of our little city, amid other vast silent houses inhabited by people I loathe without having to meet them.

"What are you doing among our enemies, Werner?" I said the first day.

"Our enemies?" said Werner, not understanding.

"For you, Werner, everything's always been easy," I told him, severely.

His bright eye is veiled by the distant, circumspect, genteel fog with which he repels any remark he might find embarrassing for me, and then I recall that, even when I was his teacher, one slightly dimmed glance could immediately make me feel all the mediocrity of my origins, all my innate lack of finesse.

"Séverine will never come to this neighborhood," I say crossly. "And besides, what can you possibly want with Séverine now?"

"I love her, and I want to live with her," Werner says serenely.

But I see his upper lip trembling. This troubles me. I hadn't expected to hear such words from his lips. I'm troubled, upset.

"Séverine should have waited for me, and, as you see," says Werner, "she didn't."

"Séverine is lugubrious," I say. "What a grim woman! Séverine, Werner, is not sexy in any way."

"No, Séverine isn't sexy," says Werner.

Again, in his eyes, that sort of mist that at least partially shields him from my foolishness and vulgarity. It hurts me, it leaves me broken. For there is nothing in Werner to find fault with. Looking away, I grumble:

"Séverine is lazy. She's kept eight of my books for fifteen years. She spends all her time on the phone. Séverine is not nice, Werner. She has nothing in her head. Séverine picks the wrong enemies and chooses her friends badly. She's aging too quickly. Oh, she's not an attractive young girl anymore, Werner. She's turning fat and doughy. I don't think Séverine deserves any better than the life she has now. What is this Séverine, deep down? A small person, savage and blind."

Werner mutters to himself in irritation, standing a safe distance from my armchair. Then I reflect that the shop teacher raising my children must know Werner's parents, as I've sometimes seen him entering their house, on Sunday, at the aperitif hour. Which means that my children, in a sense...

"You don't know Séverine," Werner says sharply.

Over the years he came back several times, solely to see Séverine. She didn't want to go to Paris. She's never gone to Paris. And now, after years of study, he's given up and left Paris for good, only to find her married to the Arab. He can't understand it. He won't resign himself to it. For Séverine was once his, Werner's, more or less officially. What does this mean? That the Arab cast a spell on her? He can't resign himself. He refuses to believe that Séverine could truly have chosen to marry the Arab. For what reason? What sense does that make?

"Séverine told me she loves him," I declare.

"Séverine told me she loved me," Werner growls, with a sinister, determined air that makes me uneasy.

He shakes his head slowly. In Paris, he then adds, he met all sorts of girls. But none had Séverine's obscure, almost unbearable appeal, which has to do with the fact that she seems to imbue herself with existence only via the purifying element of a stern, grave demeanor, austerely and instinctively demanding, of which she herself has no idea.

"Séverine doesn't run in your circles," I say, full of spite.

"No matter, since Séverine is a religious woman," Werner says calmly.

"Pff!"

Overcome with disgust, indignation, I can scarcely stop myself spitting on Werner's white wooden floor. And all at once the lush, well-tended greenery I see in the garden seems corrupted in my eyes.

Now they're all three in my house, obediently drawn here by an innocent invitation tendered and signed by the house itself—so I suppose, seeing them there, unable to imagine them showing up at my simple request. If my house schemes, can it not sometimes and by chance scheme in harmony with my desires?

They're all here, my three former students: Séverine, the Arab, Werner, still so young in my eyes that I find it difficult to believe they're as old as I was when I taught them. What sort of gratitude can I expect from these three? None, none, I tell myself, though unable to accept it entirely. And because the day before I spotted my two sons in equestrian garb in the street, because that attire and all that it signifies so scandalized me that I nearly, having no right to do so, went and rang the bell at my wife and the shop teacher's house to tell them just what I think of a good upbringing cynically pushed to such an extreme, I spontaneously place myself closer to Séverine and the Arab than to Werner.

Séverine's face furrowed with surprise on seeing Werner enter my living room. She defensively moved her hand toward her telephone, then gave up on that idea. Who was she thinking of calling for help? I wonder. My wife? Sentiments hostile to Séverine agglomerate in my mouth, forming a little ball of bitter paste, difficult to choke back. Then, as if planned out in advance, Séverine and the Arab square their shoulders. Their two faces look much alike. They stand straight and self-sufficient, unaware of their arrogance.

Werner tries to come closer to Séverine, but he stops, terror-struck, two meters away. The other two look at him, puzzled, ever so slightly repulsed, haughty and daunting. Their faces are similar, remote, radiating a haughty morality.

"I fear Séverine and her husband don't live in the same century as we do," I say to Werner with an urbane little laugh.

"Séverine, I've come back for you," says Werner.

"This fine young man..." I say, eager to tout Werner in spite of it all.

But no one hears my wispy voice, and no one pays any mind. I'm nowhere at all anymore. My house belongs to them, and all my belongings. Similarly, whenever I happen to bellow the shop teacher's name in the break room, he turns to me with a curious, affable air—and have I not then, instead, murmured entreatingly: "Oh, if you would,..." Or else, perhaps: "I wonder if you could tell me..."

Werner is red-faced and tense, hackles raised. He's dressed in an elegant, pale blue shirt, a little tight at the neck. Séverine and the Arab are wearing well-pressed sports clothes. Werner's right foot beats a distraught tattoo on my floor.

Then Séverine tells Werner his return means nothing to her. She tells Werner she's married to this other man, and everything is just as it should be. Séverine says all this to Werner in a coolly confident voice, with no cruelty intended. But how to endure such a thing? Séverine and the Arab stand shoulder to shoulder, with their matching faces, their unfounded superiority, consecrating the occupation of my house.

Fist out, I leap at Séverine. She backs away, staggering, but she doesn't fall, and she doesn't speak a word. Séverine is strong and hard. The Arab pins my arms behind me and throws me to the floor. He kicks me several times, cautious and restrained, while, as if from another time, another age, I hear Werner's anxious cries, and while, thinking what a grievous mistake it is, and how senseless, to seem to be taking his side against them, I tell myself with infinite regret that it will take far more than a rebuke such as this to get rid of me. It would take a great deal more than that.

I think I hear myself crying out:

"Take my house! Take my children! Take it all!"

My intestines are gurgling. Is that disagreeable sound drowning out my voice? Séverine hisses that I've probably broken her nose. Icily, she tells Werner not to touch her.

"We've got to get rid of the Arab," says Werner.

"We've got to get rid of me," I murmur.

"We've got to liquidate him," Werner proclaims, gripped by a sort of frenzy.

He throws himself down in one corner of my big,

desolate living room and begins to groan, head between his knees. He shows no concern for my condition. Who ever cares about his old teacher? Even when they're thirty years old, I tell myself, the students think themselves caught up in the whirlwind of life, whereas nothing vigorous or enviable seems to have grazed the existence of their teacher, still mired in the same school after so many years.

I hoist myself onto the couch. My bones hurt. Werner hiccups that he's been betrayed even more grievously than he thought, and not only Séverine but the Arab too has betrayed him, by taking a place he knew to be Werner's. No, Séverine didn't betray him. The Arab took her, bound her, such that Séverine has now lost... her freedom of choice, her will, everything she...

"Her husband works at the post office," I say.

I'm buffeted by Werner's long growl of contempt. But, in the end, is all this real? And in what way does it concern me, me to whom everyone involved owes such a great debt of patience, of understanding, of self-abnegation?

"Not to mention the books that were lent out and never returned," I say.

"We've got to get rid of him," Werner barks.

Is he going to say it? Place the burden of that mission in the hands of his former teacher?

I keep Werner with me as long as I can, dreading the moment when the darkness in my house turns sneering and vicious. I have nothing left. What I've come to realize, in a violent, blinding blaze of insight, what was conveyed to me by the unbridgeable gap separating Werner from the two others, that gap so coolly marked out by Séverine's alien, neutral voice, what all that told me, taught me, proclaimed to me, is that I will never prevent my children from riding horseback in their ridiculous getups, never bring about the return of anyone at all to my house, never again see those days when I could hope that disgrace and despair would not irrupt into my life—and that my wife and my children now have ambitions and joys entirely independent of my existence, desires that would in fact be no different if I'd died long before. Oh, it's all in the past, I tell myself, and everything's happened outside of me. For did I not furtively hope that on coming home from school one evening I might find not a disapproving, sibylline Séverine but the wife and two sons who are the true masters of this house, all three of them there in the brightly-lit living room? Bringing Séverine into my house left me no less alone. Séverine's presence was meant to remind me that I will never be young again, and at the same time that nothing, ever, will be forgiven me.

I secretly make my way into the post office, and a forgotten detail surfaces in my memory. The moment I see his pitying gaze turned toward me, I realize Séverine's husband's first name is Jamel. That gaze, I tell him within myself, seals your doom.

It's a tidy little apartment building not far from the school, on the edge of the city, and no sooner have I rung the bell than a pretty little girl with watchful eyes cracks open the door. She asks me to take off my shoes, and when I leave them on the landing she nimbly snatches them up and sets them inside, explaining that nice shoes are always liable to be stolen. I question her:

"Are you Jamel's little sister? Where's your mother? Your father? Do you work hard in school? Is your teacher happy with you?"

I glide in my stocking feet into the dining room, tiny and well-polished, filled with flowers and framed photographs, among which, again and again, I see Séverine's husband. A woman watching television stands up and turns off the set. She smiles tentatively when I introduce myself as Jamel's former teacher, turns to the little girl translating my words, then turns back to me with a congenial, almost joyful air. She gestures an invitation to take a seat at the table and sits down across from me, waiting serenely. My throat is tied in knots. Poor, poor woman, I tell myself. I sigh and yawn, forcing myself to smile at the mother all the same. Her black hair gleams at her cheeks. She waits, tranquil, untouched by doubt. Finally the little girl leaves the room. I lean toward the mother, fix my tear-filled eyes on her face, and tell her what's going to happen to her son, while, smiling and calm, trusting in the teacher, she gently nods her head, not understanding.

THE DEATH OF
CLAUDE FRANÇOIS

She then said, too quickly, trying to conceal her unease, her excitement:

"I don't see anything."

"You don't see anything?"

"Nothing at all," she said, trembling a little.

"You ought to see something."

And the woman who looked like Marlène Vador, and who was Marlène Vador, since she'd said so, added, teasing and vaguely put out:

"Well, there's something there, Doctor Zaka, so you ought to see it."

"But I'm looking, and there's nothing there, so there's nothing there."

She told herself she was glad there was nothing to look at more closely, as two minutes before she'd made precisely that claim without taking the time to be sure, so extraordinary, almost so frightening, did she find it to be examining Marlène Vador's bare back, thirty years on.

Her cheeks burning and moist, she cautiously asked:

"What happened?"

"My son shoved me into... I don't know... the corner of the sideboard, maybe. Not on purpose, of course."

"Of course," she said.

"You don't know the first thing about it," said Marlène Vador. "But I do, and I'm telling you. You remember the apartment? It's so small. A big, strapping young man knocks into his mother every day and doesn't even know it, just moving around the room, taking a breath, putting on his jacket."

"Yes. A strapping young man."

"It all goes so fast," said Marlène Vador in a dreamy, pleased voice.

She bowed her head, lowered the hand pinning her lush, unchanged mass of dark hair to her temples. The locks slipped over Marlène Vador's smooth, dusky back, hiding her satiny bra straps, but she still didn't stand up.

Doctor Zaka patted her own chest with one hand.

Did Vador need to know how furiously her, Zaka's, heart was pounding?

Back then, they'd always agreed that Marlène had a greater capacity for seeing and understanding a certain sort of mystery. Vador was a year older. Her parents were divorced. In the evening, her mother left her on her own and went out to have fun, brimming with naïve confidence and enthusiasm, and then came home very late, noisily, not always alone, to find a perfectly calm and idle Marlène waiting in the tiny kitchen, and that ten-year-old Marlène Vador smiled at her mother, relieved her of her high heels, her purse, skillfully wiped the makeup from her pretty face, put her to bed, and discreetly disappeared.

But today it was Marlène Vador revealing her flesh to Zaka and asking her opinion, although with some condescension. She was wearing a red bra embroidered with little black arrows.

Did she put that on for my sake? Zaka wondered.

Marlène sat still on the examination chair as Zaka looked down, pressing her thumbs into various spots around her waist, up her spine. Marlène Vador's flesh was supple, solid, quite thin, her bones slight and rounded. With a hesitant hand, Zaka pushed aside the locks to palpate her upper back. A shiver ran down Marlène Vador's vertebrae, and her glistening, electric hair flittered around Zaka's hands. Those clammy, fumbling hands had taken on a mind of their own, Zaka realized in disgust.

Vador jumped up and briskly pulled on the tee-shirt she'd been holding in her lap.

"That's enough for today," said Vador, impatient.

And Doctor Zaka had time to observe that Marlène's breasts were very pale beneath the red lace, and that one of those breasts bore a number of perfectly round little scars.

There was one thing Vador didn't know, she told herself. They hadn't set eyes on each other for some thirty years, neither had any idea of the life led by the other. But, Zaka told herself again, there was one thing Vador didn't know, something miraculous like nothing else.

Zaka narrowed her eyes. She bit the inside of her cheeks to keep quiet. Then, her legs trembling and weak, she cautiously sat down on the chair Vador had just vacated.

"So you still live there?" Zaka asked.

"I promised never to leave. I've never left."

Marlène Vador looked down severely at Zaka.

"You promised too, right? Remember?"

"Promised who?"

Zaka knew perfectly well. Her voice was nothing more than a whisper. Vador gave her a cold, acid little smile, and Zaka blushed violently as she thought to herself, abashed: she came all this way.

"You know perfectly well," Marlène said, very softly.

The head of a wolfhound hovered on the tee-shirt just beside Zaka's face, and she thought she heard Marlène Vador's low voice coming from the muzzle of that beast, whose eyes were so black as to bear no expression, like Marlène's own. Marlène was wearing close-cut red pants, high-heeled backless sandals, glasses with spangled frames. She gave Zaka a feeling of timeworn flash, of freshness long since faded, but in which Vador still believed with enough untroubled faith to counter the impression she made—so long admired and stunning, Vador's self-assurance seemed to assert that her beauty and charm were henceforth beyond doubt. Was she beautiful? Oh yes, Zaka said to herself, a shiver running over her flesh, she had to be. Yes, she was, she thought, before Vador's inexpressive gaze, her iris so wide that it left almost no room for the white of her eye.

She took a breath, then whispered:

"I have something amazing to. . ."

But Vador broke in, her voice now timid and pious:

"You were never much of a student, and now here you

are a doctor. I'll bet it took all you had."

"That's right," said Zaka, uncomfortable for Marlène.

She knew she was now supposed to ask "What about you?" But she had no wish to know what Vador had been up to, sensing that such talk would bring her nothing but boredom and dreariness.

Marlène Vador picked up her bag and her little red jacket. Then, Zaka told herself, she'd obviously gone on her way, slender and light, since she was no longer in the office when Zaka lowered the hand that she'd briefly laid over her eyes to shield them from the memory of something radiant and dazzling.

Doctor Zaka headed downstairs and out into the street's wilting heat.

Sweat began to flow over her forehead, and her unquiet thoughts turned to another still, stifling summer, and a day when she'd seen her mother's nape, and the napes of all the other mothers gathered on the lawn, suddenly bathed in the perspiration of horror and grief.

And now Doctor Zaka felt that same damp warmth down her neck as she hurried along the sidewalk toward the school.

How ridiculous, she told herself, all that sniveling, all that sweat, all that sorrow simply because a man had died, a perfect stranger to every one of those women on the lawn, although dearer to their wanting hearts than the many children they'd borne, than the husbands who had begotten them, whose eyes stayed dry on the death of that luminous, splendid stranger, so French, so blue-eyed, so blond-headed. A man had died, and Zaka's mother was never the same again. She knew everything about that man, and that man had no idea she existed, but with that man's essence Zaka's mother had fueled her raging need to love with abundance and selflessness. Pitted against the glory, the magnetism of the French tongue so gracefully wielded, what hope was there for Zaka's father, or any of the other fathers, with their dingy words?

Zaka's mother never recovered. Had she glimpsed even the first stirring of a recovery, Zaka told herself, she would have violently crushed it out. None of the mothers wanted to be unburdened of their grief. What would be left, once they'd given up their sadness?

Doctor Zaka stopped before the iron bars of the school's fence. In the fierce heat, the school wavered faintly before her eyes. She saw her daughter's father slowly approaching, sweat streaming down his bloated face, his pants resting very low on his hips, held down by his pot belly. Their eyes met, and he blanched. A puff of contempt inflated Zaka's lips. She shook her head no, her eyes cold, half-shut.

This wasn't his week to pick up the child from school. He knew that, she could see it. So fierce was her hatred for this man that for a moment she thought it had blinded her, or that all this—the school, the fence, the ex-husband with the bulging bags under his eyes—had blown away on a whirlwind of rage. It was to see her, Zaka, that he'd come here today, because he couldn't care less about the child, whom he never quite knew what to do with when he did have her.

Now she could see him again, pale and huge.

He was backing away, disappointed, eyeing Zaka with a gaze he tried to fill with deep and irrevocable meaning, but which was only plaintive, she thought, embarrassed to see him still there, reminding her of what she'd had to do to conceive her little girl.

She'd coupled with a white elephant, and that generous but slow-witted animal wouldn't give up on the idea that it was her equal.

Doctor Zaka let out a strident laugh. People turned and stared. She took out a handkerchief, ran it over her short, thick, blond and gray hair, over her trickling nape.

Let them stare. They had no idea of the freakish intimacy that had taken place between the abject blimp now trudging away and herself, so poised and so lively, taut and unchanged, and no idea, what's more, that to this day she remained an object of that stubborn elephant's grimy affections.

Let them stare. Another sharp yelp escaped her. She felt cruel, unhinged, but stronger than all of them, snugly encased in a sheath of sarcasm and hardness from which Vador herself, that afternoon, could not have extracted her. She knew all about Vador's virtue; she knew why, standing there before her, she'd so strongly felt her own betrayal, her failing.

It had to do with the death of Claude François. But it made absolutely no sense.

Doctor Zaka gently shook her head.

It made absolutely no sense.

And yet, on the pretext of an invented injury, Marlène Vador had come all the way to the center of Paris from the ragged-lawned suburban town where they'd once lived, simply to shame her for not keeping her word—or was that not it at all? Whatever it was, Marlène still didn't know that Zaka had more than redeemed herself for anything she might hold against her.

But what about the death of Claude François?

Zaka was quivering faintly. Her metal sheath quivered along with her.

Though only a child at the time, Vador too had sternly rebuffed all thoughts of consolation, firmly resolved that the death of Claude François would be the epicenter of all her life's upheavals, a life then in existence for only twelve years. And, Zaka remembered, there were so many women in their little housing project who had scrupulously honored their vow of eternal mourning, despite the passing years, despite the emergence of new, still handsomer singers.

They'd stood there, sweating and petrified, outside the apartment building. News of the death had drifted from a neighbor's open window. One of them let out a moan— Zaka's mother? Vador's mother?

Vador's mother hadn't kept her word.

Then they were all weeping, crying out: no, it can't be...

Did Marlène really faint, or was Zaka making that up, there before the school gate, in the heat rising from the softening asphalt?

There was no doubt about it: Marlène had fainted.

Zaka felt stinging tears in her eyes.

Then the mothers were sad, and the children fell into a blank, jealous stupor.

Vador's fickle, adorable mother alone soon developed a passion for another singer. But not Zaka's mother, nor Zaka nor Marlène, and Marlène, in a sense, less than anyone. They took to praying each day for the repose of Claude François's soul.

Zaka discreetly prodded her eyelids with both fists.

The mothers seemed reluctant to leave the lawn and go back to their apartments. They lingered, vacant and drained, stamping the dry grass with a solitude, a defeat, and an incomprehension so overwhelming that the children, afraid and unsettled, stole away from that yellowing patch, sat down on the sidewalk beside it, dully watching the clogged or slippered feet trampling what tomb? what body? in a desperate jig of love, the slender, pale, lightly freckled ankles of their mothers, still young, now suddenly unrecognizable. Zaka remembered that Claude François's death shrouded the housing project in a melancholy with no escape.

All at once the girl was standing before her. Zaka let out a little cry:

"Paula!"

Then, in a tone of tender reproach:

"Where did you come from? Hey, Paula! Oh, for…"

The child said nothing. She was watching something behind Zaka's back, something that bent her mouth into a half-smile. A light glaze of sweat glistened on her forehead. Zaka turned around slowly, cautiously, lest a careless movement jar the invisible, protective sheath. She saw Paula's father, standing motionless not far behind her. Dizzy with rage, she shouted:

"Will you go away? Will you get out of here? What do you want?"

"Shh, mama. It's OK, he's going now, poor papa. You don't have to talk so loud."

"It's just that stupid elephant, getting me all worked up. I don't like that, I don't like it one bit."

She was still shouting, in spite of herself. She forced herself to keep quiet. She could hear her watch crystal clicking against the metal of her sheath, but she knew she was the only one who could hear it.

"You don't have to call him an elephant in front of all these people."

The air whistled between Paula's teeth. Zaka lifted her chin with one outstretched finger, and the girl looked up at her with Marlène Vador's marvelous face.

"How I love you," cried Zaka, charmed, proud, unbelieving.

A jolt of pain pierced the back of her head. She fell to the sidewalk, not slumping but toppling, stiff and firm in her armor.

Doctor Zaka and her daughter Paula took a bus line unknown to them both. They got off at the last stop, as far into the suburbs of Paris as they'd ever been. Paula had refused to take a window seat. And when Zaka gaily pointed out all the changes the place had seen since her childhood, her daughter Paula answered only with a noncommittal flexing of her very red lips (red as Vador's lipsticked lips, and not a trace of rouge, Zaka repeated to herself reflexively) and a polite nod, never looking at her or so much as glancing outside.

Off the bus, she kept that same impregnable halo of coldness around her.

Zaka wondered if the child was afraid. Or was she, like herself, her mother Zaka, walking down this street in a protective sheath that she feared might ring out if tapped by her fingernails or belt buckle?

Zaka had advised Paula on the clothes she should wear for this outing. She examined the little girl with pleasure and surprise. Paula was dressed as Marlène was no doubt in the habit of dressing: a clinging tee-shirt printed with fuchsia scorpions, so tiny and numerous that you had to squint to withstand the sight of them, and a pair of tight, very light-colored jeans, cinched with an alligator-print belt. On the child's feet, high-heeled boots of cream-colored canvas, specially purchased by Zaka for their trip to the outer suburbs.

She was quite aware that Paula was not of an age to be dressed in this way.

Oh yes, she knew that.

She smiled at herself, a little stiffly, but who would dare claim that she dressed her daughter in such clothes for music lessons or school? Not even the unpleasant man who happened to be the child's father could deny that Paula's very busy little social life unfolded against a background of muted shades and full, classic cuts, that they were both, mother and daughter alike, true bourgeoises, refined and invisible. Zaka was not in the habit of showing off Paula's beauty.

But was it her fault if Marlène Vador did not have the same tastes, the same ways?

Paula's long black hair clapped gently against her slender back.

"Where are we going?" she asked quietly.

"To visit a friend."

Zaka put on a cheery voice—what was Paula afraid of, here in the very neighborhood where her mother had grown up? Why was her daughter afraid, with Marlène Vador's features on her face?

"You have a friend here?"

"My best friend, even if it's been thirty years since I last saw her. And why, if you please, shouldn't I have a friend here, and even a very good friend?"

She saw a little muscle twitching on Paula's cheek. How pale the child was today, and how tense! Zaka began to fear she might not carry this off, or perhaps she'd been wrong from the start. Paula staggered on her platform soles. Zaka steadied her, eyeing her closely, that little-girl face so unlike her own, and nothing like her husband's, but in every way, by the grace of a chemistry of prayers and calculations, like a stranger's. She was annoyed by the child's apprehensions. She herself once lived in this place—it wasn't right to be afraid.

On her own face, Doctor Zaka plastered a resolutely carefree expression. She wasn't beautiful, she was rough and angular, but was she not an accommodating person? She took Paula's arm and, slowly caressing the hollow of her elbow, did her best to look around through her daughter's eyes.

"You're not too cold? My little one! Maybe you're hungry? You want something to eat? Do you want a roll, a brioche?"

She went on and on, not even hearing herself speak.

Overwrought, she squeezed Paula's arm a little too hard, and the child politely pulled free.

How could she deny it, how could she deny it? And shame fogged her glasses' thick lenses. From Paula's lost, dismayed air, she could see what had become of the street she'd so often walked with Vador at her side, from the housing project to the junior high, and that narrow street was once lined with tidy little homes, low apartment houses with flowers in windowboxes, not, oh no, these blighted gray concrete buildings, doors and windows closed off with plywood or cinderblocks, courtyards congested with trash. Two video clubs and a dusty-windowed sex shop, perhaps open, perhaps out of business, had replaced... Zaka couldn't recall what.

"I think there was a bakery around here somewhere. Do you want to find a bakery? If my little one wants something to eat, then we'll find a bakery..."

"I don't want anything," Paula whispered.

"In my day, there were two or three bakeries just in this neighborhood."

Her tone was almost pleading. How to believe someone could walk down a street such as this every day and then, much later, give birth to a girl like Paula? If Paula refused to believe it, that was only common sense.

Zaka felt cruelly humiliated. How stupid of her to try to take pride in the life she'd led here, in this drab disaster! She touched the thick bandage swaddling the back of her head.

"Does it hurt?" asked Paula, anxious.

"Yes."

"You shouldn't have been so mean to him."

Paula stopped to look at her, eyes dilated with fear.

"You're right," mumbled Zaka, forcing a deferential grimace.

"Wouldn't you have thrown a rock at him if he'd talked to you like that?"

"You're right, I would have thrown a rock at him."

She almost added "that fat animal," but she managed to choke back those words, which would have hurt Paula (and why could her daughter find no better cause for compassion than her idiot father, why?). Instead, with a mocking snort aimed at gaining the child's complicity, she quickly added:

"I would have thrown a much bigger rock than he did, but would that have been enough to flatten him?"

"I'm sick of this!" Paula shouted.

"You're right, honey," said Zaka, putting her arms around her.

Tenderly pressing the small of her back, she started Paula walking again.

"You want something to eat? You want a little bun? A brioche?"

"I'm sick of this," Paula murmured, distant and unhostile, as if to herself.

A little later, she asked the child to wait in front of the building, where there was still a vast playground. The sand was much dirtier and more meager than she remembered. Doctor Zaka felt the inside of her mouth go dry.

"You can play, but don't get dirty," she said with some effort.

Then she remembered: Paula had stopped playing in the sand long ago.

Lips oddly downturned, Paula told her she didn't want to stay in this place by herself.

"When I was your age," said Zaka, "I spent all day outside, right here where we're standing."

She kissed her daughter and walked off toward the front door, its cracked pane of glass patched with brown packing tape, here reflecting scattered pieces of stormy gray sky, the sign of a heavy, hot rain soon to come, there reflecting—or was she mistaken?—Paula's face, imprisoned in a broken triangular shard, so creased and distorted by panic as to seem shrunken, crumpled around a gaping mouth that might, at any moment, open into a bellow of fear.

"I'll call you when it's time, and you can come up and join me," said Zaka.

She hadn't turned around. She was talking to the door, the reflection. Paula couldn't hear her.

She walked into the lobby, still just as she remembered it.

Vador was so beautiful.

She'd traded her glittering glasses for a pair of tinted contact lenses. At first Doctor Zaka was stunned to see her with blue eyes. How could I have foreseen contact lenses? Poor Paula…Then, like a small explosion, a certainty resounded between the walls of her throbbing skull: the color of her eyes made no difference. Nor did it in any way matter that Vador had appeared in the doorway wearing a genteel, ladylike, longish, beige cotton skirt and a white, round-collared blouse with mother of pearl buttons. Her hair was tied back behind her neck, and straight bangs covered her forehead down to the two periwinkle blue marbles standing in (temporarily? Zaka hoped so) for her eyes, which were in reality of the same brown as Paula's.

This was not the Marlène she'd so often seen, in her thoughts as in her dreams, welcoming her into her home, first surprised, then delighted, just as she was now. She'd imagined a Marlène whose tinge of vulgarity she'd have to try to overlook, her overeagerness to display her body—traits, Zaka reflected, that she might have shared had she stayed on and lived here.

Vador was so beautiful.

Today she's middle-class and magnificent, Zaka told herself, intimidated.

"You kept your mother's apartment."

"Yes. Mama died here," said Vador, as if that explained it.

"It wasn't for Claude François' sake?"

Zaka had leapt right in. To her immediate regret, a sort of titter escaped her. But Marlène's thin face lit up, as if illuminated from within, from just beneath her fine, dusky skin.

She said to Zaka:

"I thought you'd forgotten him."

"Why?" asked Zaka, slightly insulted.

"You went away. You live in Paris. We swore we'd stay here. But I'm the only one. The whole neighborhood's forgotten Claude François."

What could Zaka say, faced with those eyes? She went

and looked out the living-room window. Far below, she saw Paula's motionless little head, then thick drops of rain began to fall and the child's head disappeared. A warm smell came up to meet Zaka, rising from the sand, from the dust in the steaming parking lot. She's gone to find shelter, she told herself, vaguely concerned.

She was standing in Vador's living room, and she recognized the furniture Vador's mother had cluttered it with long before. Her first impression, that Marlène had kept everything just as it was, was oddly reinforced by the unexpected presence of a small round side table and a crushed velvet armchair that stirred up an aged layer of mud deep in Zaka's heart. She ran one hesitant finger over the table's varnished top.

"That comes from your place," said Marlène.

She flashed a triumphant little smile.

"Your mother gave it to mine, along with the armchair and a bunch of other stuff I finally had to sell."

Zaka smiled into space. What was Marlène trying to distract her from with this tedious talk of furniture? And how could she, Zaka, possibly have once lived with such furniture, and found it nice and even rather chic?

Rain was spattering against the windowpanes. Everything had gone very dark.

Zaka saw Marlène Vador's artificial eyes shining. And all around there were dozens of similar pairs of eyes, some of them huge, on the living room wall, others more modest, in picture frames lined up on the sideboard, on the TV set, or, in close ranks, on two or three chairs sacrificed for their display. Zaka knew most of the photos. She'd helped Marlène cut them out, long ago, from magazines bought for precisely that purpose.

And today Marlène had given herself the same eyes as Claude François.

A lump clogged Zaka's throat. She rushed to Marlène and embraced her. How long had it been since she last clasped a full-sized adult body in her arms? Oh, years and years, she thought. A sort of euphoria came over her. Vador's torso felt bony and cold, but all the same, how wonderful to embrace a substantial body, on the same scale as one's own!

She felt an urge to nestle her head against Marlène's neck, inhale its open-hearted scent of soap, but she didn't dare, though she thought she could feel her friend's muscles relaxing—and she was indeed her friend, she'd known that all through those thirty years she'd pretended to forget it.

"You're the best friend I ever had. We'll be seeing a lot of each other from now on. Right? Right?"

"No, not a lot. I'm going to die soon."

Zaka loosened her grasp. She pulled back, arms outstretched, to look at Marlène.

In spite of her refashioned gaze, Vador was so beautiful.

"And why on earth should you be dying anytime soon?" cried Zaka, frowning and jovial.

She sometimes addressed the doleful old ladies who came to her office in exactly this way.

"I've made up my mind to," Vador murmured.

She motioned quickly toward the innumerable faces of Claude François. Her delicate nostrils clenched.

"In a month, it will be twenty-five years since he died. I don't want to live any longer than he did. We made a vow about that, too. You remember?"

Zaka went back to the window and opened it in spite of the rain, which immediately began to spray Vador's little living room and her own flushed face, her big, black-framed glasses. In a distraught voice, she called out:

"Paula!"

What good was her miracle now? What good, now, were her fearless life and her offering to Vador?

She closed the window and turned around to see Marlène calmly wiping raindrops from the pictures with a chamois.

"That's why I came to your office," said Marlène in a low, gentle voice. "To ask for your help, because I don't know how to do it."

"My daughter Paula's downstairs... She'll be up soon... You'll meet her..."

"Oh, at this point, I don't..."

"You'll recognize her... You're my friend..."

"What great friends we were, you remember?"

And Marlène let out a sad little laugh, giving Zaka, whose face was trickling wet from the rain, a glance of such tender, unexpected companionship that Zaka couldn't hold back a surge of pleasure. Vador put the last picture back in its place, now thoroughly dried. She caressed Claude François's cheek with one wrist, lovingly, reflexively, as, Zaka thought, she must have been doing for decades, every day, several times a day.

"In the end," said Vador, "he will have been my only love."

Then, before Zaka could tell where it had come from, she found herself holding a photograph, and she heard Marlène explaining all sorts of things she had no wish to know of, and already, inside her, the obscure guardian of her serenity was fighting off all awareness of them.

But that these two embittered, confused-looking old people in the photo Vador had thrust into her hands—that these two forlorn, heartbreaking old people were her own parents, Zaka, caught off guard, could not help but see.

"Because they thought you really had died, poor things, and they would have been so happy if they'd known you were a doctor, but I looked after them to the end, along with my mother, and that, it turns out, was my youth, on one side those three old people, and on the other my passion, my passion..."

"And that son of yours..." Zaka choked out.

"No, I don't have a son, I don't have any children."

"But you told me you had a son."

"I never said that."

Vador pursed her lovely plump lips in indignation. She let out a short laugh, authoritarian, disapproving.

"How can you say such a thing? That I said... My poor Zaka."

"You told me. I remember it clearly."

Vador shrugged and took back the old couple's picture, which Zaka, unaware, was about to drop onto the carpet. With a pious, loving attention that Zaka found all the more disturbing because it seemed to her wholly sincere, she leaned the photo against one of the framed pictures, the one that showed Claude François running through a glorious meadow with his two sons.

What envy, and even what jealousy, Zaka suddenly recalled, that picture had injected into their fervent, devoted little-girl emotions, the day they cut it out and glued it to a piece of cardboard! For they were exactly the right age to be Claude François's children, the two daughters he might have had, one of them beautiful and one ugly. Then they began to imagine they really were Claude François's daughters—had they not gone so far as to glue their own faces over those of the two boys who had unjustly supplanted them in that sublime role?

Hoping to patch things up, she was about to ask Marlène if she remembered being Claude François's pretty older daughter, when something in the curve of Marlène's back as she bent over her, Zaka's, parents (long dead, shoved aside with hostility and derision) suddenly revealed to her how much kinder Marlène Vador was than she—how incomparably better, how incontestably more compassionate than she herself had ever been. All at once her eyes filled with tears.

"I can't do what you're asking," said Zaka.

"I'll manage," said Marlène.

"I would so much have liked for us to see each other again."

Vador smiled, regretful, resolute, infinitely sad. She stood there in her polished, dowdy little living room, her face as if pierced in two places by the gleam of her immortal eyes, her arms limp at her sides, and Zaka knew that this woman was no longer her friend. And for all her exemplary kindliness, this woman who was no longer her friend would never be moved by anything that might happen to Zaka. It was all over, it had all come to an end, long before Zaka could have imagined.

Zaka stepped forward and quickly hugged Marlène Vador, who was, in a way, no longer Marlène Vador.

Who was it that had cried out, with a furious, desperate, bewildered sob: "It's all over, we'll never meet him!"?

Maybe Zaka's mother, maybe Vador's. Not Marlène, certainly not, her eyes half closed onto the comforting, mysterious certainty that she would indeed meet him one day, that nothing was ever over as long as you weren't dead yourself.

Doctor Zaka bustled back and forth in front of the apartment building, calling:

"Paula! Paula!"

She ran through the puddles, ungainly. She was fat and graceless, and no imaginary sheath or metal casing could protect her now. She was ashamed to have played at thinking herself light and hard when she was so ponderous, so broad. And now her daughter Paula was nowhere to be seen, and it was her fault. And the back of her head was throbbing. And how could she not remember the shocked shout that had burst from Vador's lips as Zaka bolted out of the room, alarmed that Paula hadn't come up:

"You can't leave a child alone around here anymore!"

Oh, Marlène Vador would never see the little girl who had Marlène Vador's face—for that too, it was too late. And what was Marlène Vador's face now, since that woman was no longer a friend, since nothing mattered to her anymore but not exceeding Claude François' lifespan?

Now Zaka's cheeks were bathed in tears. She trundled along, unsure which way to turn. The flesh jiggled on her hips and her arms.

"Paula! Paula!"

Her glasses slipped off her nose. At the same instant, Zaka made an awkward leap from the street to the sidewalk. She heard the lenses shatter underfoot, and she would have liked to make a similar noise, the stinging expression of her despair and her terror.

Trembling, she picked up the glasses.

"Oh God, oh God."

She stuffed the mangled frames into her pocket and tried to look around, squinting. Suddenly, among the tall, run-down towers—so like the one that Marlène still lived in, that Zaka herself had once lived in, when those buildings took the luminous, white, well-tended form of their childhood—she thought she spotted Paula's small fuchsia figure. She believed she could make out another vague shape beside her, and she warily started forward again, panting loudly, unsure if she should call out. Another wave of pain drilled into her head, and as she winced, pulling back her upper lip, the figure at Paula's side turned away. Zaka thought she recognized the child's father. And although a bitter substance immediately filled her mouth, she was ashamed to have pretended to see Paula's father as a huge, flabby man, cowardly and deceit-ful. She realized she could keep that ruse up no longer. She wanted to spit at his back—but how not to see, despite her nearsightedness, that he had the proudly erect back of a fine and upstanding man? That man had stopped loving her long before: long, long before. Would he love her again if, one hand very visibly pressed to her bandage, she shrieked:

"What are you doing here? I'll see you in court!"

And she, Zaka, would she stop loving him, in spite of it all? What did she have to do, she wondered, her head spinning, to turn regret and nostalgia into indifference?

She stopped and stood, exhausted. She felt her entire body shivering with desire and resentment, aimed at that man who was no longer hers, who had lost all regard for her.

Just then the man walked away with a long, relaxed stride. Now Zaka was not at all sure that he was Paula's father.

And now Paula herself, or the silhouette that might have been hers, took off as well, in the other direction. The cold shadow of a building swallowed her up.

Doctor Zaka happened onto her daughter at the bus stop.

"Mama! I was waiting for you," said Paula, joyously.

And then, seeing her daughter's eyes shining with an enthusiasm and a gaiety she'd never seen before, Zaka was embarrassed by her own naked face, glistening with despair.

She forced herself to smile, held back the words of reproach and relief.

She did her best to prepare herself: any revelation would have to be greeted with benevolence.

THE BOYS

When a woman who called herself E. Blaye showed up at the neighbors' farm, the neighbors—the four Mours—were still eating their lunch.

René watched them eat. From the dark kitchen corner, he looked on as the father's and mother's and two Mour boys' little violet mouths primly, ruefully opened to admit the pieces of eggplant their relentless forks were thrusting inside, leaving only the handles visible between the wary, unwilling, pried-open lips of the Mours and their two boys, who all glanced up together to look at the woman. Sometimes René slid over on his chair and bent his head to one side to watch the Mours' legs moving gently beneath the table, their long legs, their dainty feet in identical blue espadrilles. The Mours' eight lower limbs undulated dreamily, and all the while, up above, a battle was being waged between the stubborn mouths and the forks plunging into those mouths' most secret depths.

The Mours' four gray gazes landed as one on the visitor. René straightened up in his seat, although no one was looking his way. It was for that very reason, he knew, because no one felt obliged to pay him any mind, that they let him stay in the kitchen at lunchtime. René was hungry, but they never offered him their leftovers. He sensed that, had one of the Mours cared enough to invite him to share, he would lose his right to stay in that dark corner, nearly every day, swaying in his seat as he watched the little plum-colored mouths straining to fight off the food. Surprised and impatient, they would have said:

"Well, René? Time to go home!"

And could poor René have told them that he felt a kinship with each of those mouths, so fiercely determined to defend its purity against the perfidious temptations of meat, of any food at all? The Mours didn't realize that their lips opened only because they were forced to, only René could see that, just as he saw, tilting his head, that the Mours' consciences sided with their placid, swaying legs. René, on the other hand, knew that his whole body and mind struggled against the desire to eat, that weakness, and then that remorse. He knew more about that than the Mours.

Now the woman was explaining that she'd found the door half-open onto the heat of the farmyard, and thought there was no need to knock. She dropped a calling card onto the table and Madame Mour eagerly snatched it up to read it aloud, thereby, without seeking to, without even thinking of it, informing René that the woman's name was E. Blaye.

"We weren't expecting you so early," said Madame Mour.

"I don't have much time," said the woman. "I've got to get back to work. Let's try and make this quick."

A sort of squeal burst from the lips of the younger, handsomer, cleverer of the two Mour sons, the same age as René. He looked down at his plate and the shadow of his eyelashes veiled his cheeks, which, to his deep surprise, René had seen blushing violently. A heavy pall of discomfort filled the kitchen. But it had no effect on the woman, and René could feel her impatience, her irritation. Her gaze darted from brother to brother. It settled on Anthony, the younger, handsomer one.

"This must be him," she said, placated.

"Yes, that's him," said Madame Mour. "Did you hear? Come on, go get your bag."

And, as Anthony slowly pushed back his chair and rose without a glance at the others, the lower half of his face still dimmed by the blue shadow of his thick black eyelashes, the woman, pleased to see herself obeyed, absent-mindedly turned her attention to the rest of the room, the Mours' old-fashioned little kitchen, whose décor and amenities they'd been vowing to update for twenty years, never finding the money to do it, and which, René realized, E. Blaye was now seeing in all its clutter of yellowed furniture, brown house-wares, pitiful, valiant utensils.

How Anthony was trembling on his way out of the kitchen, René said to himself.

Young and curly-headed, the Mour father sat perfectly still. He stared at his empty plate, breathing heavily.

The woman had briefly but carefully studied Anthony Mour's lithe physique, confined in an undersized pair of pants and a tank top bearing the crest of an American basketball team, she'd watched him walk away, dragging his espadrilles with a sort of shambling haste, she'd seen, René told himself, heart pounding, Anthony Mour's grace through his fear and unease, his languidly supple movements, the nudity of his muscular arms, golden and rippling, she'd shivered with pleasure, René told himself, perhaps with relief (had she feared she might end up with the brother?). And then she'd fixed a cold eye on each of the Mours, and then on René, not seeing him, so perfectly did he blend in with the dim wall, the shabby chiaroscuro of the far end of the room.

Now she was pacing, with measured steps. Eager to be done with all this, she cast a glance out at the white, blazing farmyard each time she came to the open door, as if she needed to fill herself with fresh air or the thought of a hot, dazzling freedom before she could plunge back into the Mours' dim, rancid kitchen, or as if, René thought, the idea of fleeing crossed her mind whenever her footsteps passed from shadowed to sunlit floor tiles. She paced in her flat sandals, indiscreetly checking her watch. Across the farmyard, René saw the oblong form of a car.

"Hurry up!" Madame Mour shouted irritably.

She was yelling up toward the room Anthony had vanished into. She stood, then sat down again, indecisive, ashamed, her thin face deep crimson. The Mour father's perfect immobility and reproachful, humiliated silence undermined her assurance. Stumbling over her words, she ordered Anthony's brother to go get him. When they returned, the homelier brother was walking behind, as if to prevent Anthony from backing out, snickering a little, soundlessly, his face contorted—much like Anthony in the muscular slenderness of his limbs, the swinging indolence of his gait, the grimy old American-sports-star jersey, the espadrilles slapping his feet, the tight pants worn very low on his pelvis, but Anthony's exact opposite, and almost his antagonist, in the form of his face: shapeless, hesitant, blunt, as if seeking to parody the impeccable sharpness of Anthony's features, and managing only to make itself pathetic and vindictive.

The brother led Anthony to the woman. He laid Anthony's bag at his feet, then stood close by, keeping a discreet but vigilant watch.

Poor guy, poor guy, thought René, horrified. For the juxtaposition of those two faces, so comparable in their unlikeness, made it abundantly clear that Anthony had been chosen because he'd turned out well, while the other was an inferior product, deeply and irreparably disgraced. Devoid of commercial value, he seemed of no use, and relegated to lowly and inessential tasks: bringing his brother to the woman, remembering the bag, keeping an eye on his brother. And all this with the insincere simpering of one who strives to anticipate authority's needs, who seeks only to please that authority, and who knows that it never even sees him.

"All right, off we go," said E. Blaye, gaily.

And to Madame Mour alone, in a clear but quiet voice:

"I'll write you to arrange the payments."

The brother acknowledged this with a snort. Unable to answer, Madame Mour half closed her eyes. But René sat in the clutches of an agonizing jealousy. He looked at the Mour father in hopes of convincing himself that Anthony's situation was in no way desirable, in no way meritorious, the Mour father who sat petrified with disgust at the dishonor being done to his household, but what's the use, René asked himself, what's the use, since he wasn't the one now disappearing into the sun-drenched farmyard, no doubt leaving forever, putting the Mours' wretched kitchen behind him, since it wasn't him but handsome Anthony that a woman named E. Blaye, a woman from the city, the same age as Madame Mour but younger-looking, was closely tailing through the dusty farmyard, surely gazing at his tanned nape, his soft shoulders, enveloping Anthony's neck with the eager warmth of her breath.

"He's gone," Madame Mour murmured, coming in from the front step.

"You see how old she was?" said the brother.

And he raised his voice to a scandalized, indignant pitch, but in vain, for, René thought, he had no idea what a true scandal was.

"So?" said Madame Mour. "What difference does that make?"

Neither opening his mouth nor raising his eyes, the Mour father declared:

"You'll never talk about him again. You'll never speak his name in my house. He's dead. He's gone. We don't know who he is, where he's buried, we don't honor his memory."

That evening, René said to his mother:

"The Mours sold Anthony to a lady from town."

"For how much?"

"They didn't say."

"Good for him. He'll be happier there."

Slightly eased by the exhausting walk home on a sun-blistered road, that insistent itch of envy and spite now flooded back with new vigor, irritating every fiber of René's body and soul. He looked at his mother and realized that the mute, outraged question he was asking her (And why shouldn't you find the same sort of lady for me?) was being answered in kind, by her unhappy, resigned, realistic glance, by a small, dubious shake of the head (What have you got to sell, my son?). He couldn't help blurting out:

"I'm young, after all."

It was true, he had that, all that, but was youth without beauty, without money, without talent, emaciated youth in a tin-roofed hut hemmed in almost to the threshold by endless fields of corn that did not belong to René's mother, was youth unnoticed by all not the equivalent of the grimmest and loneliest old age? René had thought of that, he thought about it unendingly. His youth was purely theoretical. It had neither importance nor weight nor anything he might turn to his benefit. At least Anthony's brother, the homely Mour, radiated irrefutable youth from his hard, brutal body. René's own body was feeble, scrawny, and misshapen.

He watched his mother's hand slide something he didn't want to look at across the table.

"Have some. You like it"—her voice weary, hopeless, vaguely indifferent.

He gently pushed back his chair and stood up. Light-headed, he felt his knees buckling. He seized a piece of bread, stuffed it whole into his mouth, and left the house, chewing with difficulty, painfully and despairingly. My God, my God, my God. Outside the doorway, he stumbled over a mangled tricycle, his footsteps crushed pieces of plastic dishware, clothespins, fragments of dirty, rusting scrap metal.

The cool of night was finally coming. Although the sky was still light, the shadows of the cornstalks, taller than René, had already shrouded the house in a squalling violet darkness, insects, mysterious vermin. Through the invisible creatures' gratings and tiny cries, René could hear the tortured breathing and restive snores of his young brothers and sisters, sleeping together upstairs in the loft, dulled by the heat beneath the tin roof, unpacified, he could picture their little bodies, so absurdly numerous, scattered every which way on the mattresses, freckled with mosquito bites.

René thought about the bread he'd just swallowed. He hopped from foot to foot in the dim light of the cornfields, spitting out tiny crumbs as his tongue dug them out of his cheeks. A bitter self-loathing stopped him from going back inside and up to bed. How feckless he was! What a coward! Had he only, a few moments before, risen from the table brusquely and decisively, his legs would have supported the pitifully slight weight of his bones as they usually did, and he could easily have forbidden his hand to reach out for the bread. Whereas…Oh God, oh God. Was it to console his mother? Was it gluttony? Had the bread not literally leapt into his fingers? The memory of that bread strangled his stomach. He thought he could feel himself swelling up monstrously in the dark, inflated by his own cowardice. And was his mother consolable, was gluttony permissible? There was no reason, no excuse, for... René clenched his fist and hammered cruel little blows on his forehead, his ears.

He heard the sound of slinking footsteps from the path that led down to their house—for, in a spirit of solidarity, this hovel rented from the cornfields' owner could just as well become his house, their house, whenever one of those dispiriting men who sometimes and too often turned out to be the father of one of the little forms groaning upstairs in the heat, whenever one of those types in grimy polo shirts, yellow-toenailed in their plastic flipflops, decided to approach it, timidly, as if obeying some unknown convention, some etiquette, some requirement for courtliness and restraint, to pay René's mother a call that might sometimes last days, or months.

"Yeah? Who's there?" René shouted, his irritation taking his mind off himself and the memory of the bread.

His voice quavered a little, for it sometimes happened that this very question, barked out dozens of times toward the pitch-black path, met with the reply "It's your father," spoken calmly, coldly, objectively, and then the appearance of a man exactly like all the rest, in a tattered t-shirt and old khakis cut off at the knees.

Clenched and ashamed, René would see him glance quickly his way, the faint glimmer of interest in his eyes dimming at once.

And so René could never hear cracking twigs on the path without dread, fearing his father might show up again, smirking and remote, scarcely troubling to conceal his disdain for René, or at least for the René he'd just laid eyes on.

He continued to haunt the Mour's farmyard.

Every morning, after walking those of his brothers and sisters who still went to school as far as the bus stop and leaving them on the narrow strip of grass between the road and the cornstalks, he hurried onward down that same road, already hot and dry, soon seeing the bus pass him by, glimpsing his brothers' and sisters' faces pressed to the windows, their noses flattened, their eyes too close together, and raised one hand toward those unlovely faces in an attempt at a jaunty wave, thinking "They look just like me," with pity and disgust, for how was it that such varied progenitors had each time produced this same sort of child, without spark, without strength, without qualities? There was some kind of... something in that... a cruel trick, an injustice? Or else...

He stopped to rest. His head spun, his vision paled. When he finally reached the Mours' vast, tidy farmyard, his breath came heavy and rough, he was exhausted. Sometimes Madame Mour spotted him and assigned him some chore, which he took his time with, so that he could stay a while longer and try to understand what was eluding him. He refilled the four dogs' food bowl in the corner of the yard where they were chained up, or opened the old car's trunk to carry in the bags of food bought at the distant supermarket for the week to come, and meanwhile he focused all his faculties, straining to pick up any sign of a change, of a metamorphosis... of... what? What must the Mour household be like, with handsome Anthony gone? Like the surface of a still, silent water once the stone of humiliation and regret has been swallowed and forgotten? Like the surface of a water more silent than ever before?

Madame Mour would be waiting for him on the front step, arms crossed, distant and benevolent. She watched him intently, narrowing her eyes. She tucked her shoulder-length hair behind her ears and tapped the ground with the toe of her espadrille, unconcerned by the dust she kicked up.

Soon he helped Madame Mour bring in a computer and set it up on a little table in one corner of the kitchen. And when he came the next day, there was Anthony on the screen, against a background of blue sky and glass towers, amid which René thought he could make out the smiling face of the woman named E. Blaye, Anthony so handsome, so glowing, that René couldn't repress a brief groan.

"You see?" said Madame Mour, triumphant. "You see, you see?"

Had René ever doubted it? Doubted what? The spectacular radiance, the prosperity, the new ecstasy that shone in Anthony's eyes, that strewed even the sky behind him with sparkles? And the woman's face was shining as well, splashed with Anthony's magnificence.

"He sent us some money," said Madame Mour. "A lot of money, already. And I have the computer and the internet and it's just like he was here. Isn't it?"

"Oh yes," said René.

For there was no denying that Anthony seemed to be there, more than he ever had. Strangely expert, Madame Mour set a string of images flipping by on the screen, showing Anthony's face at various moments of his consecration, his triumph, in varied locales, or rather, René thought, against various backdrops, for René didn't quite believe in those American megalopolises, those Florentine villas, those Parisian restaurants against which Anthony's multiple wonderful faces stood out like illuminations, with an almost naïve sheen, always him, Anthony Mour, but more glorious in each image, more assured—still himself, to be sure, but by the end so remade that René scarcely recognized him. It seemed to him that Anthony's mouth, chin, and nose had been slightly reshaped. But he must have been wrong, because none of this surprised Madame Mour, whose eyes were crinkling with delight.

"How handsome he is, how handsome—don't you think?" she murmured.

"Yes," said René, despairing.

She passed over the next pictures more hurriedly, some of them showing Anthony fully nude, and then some of Anthony and E. Blaye as a couple, also nude, in a white-painted bedroom. René felt like he'd been punched hard in the chest. Distraught, he glanced at Madame Mour. But, bent over the screen, intent, she only stroked the backs of her ears, where her hair stayed obediently tucked. Her lower lip was slightly curled under—was she at least puzzled? René wondered. Or cautiously refraining from judgment, for the moment? Did she want to gather all the necessary elements for an explanation, and then an excuse, for…In a neutral tone, René asked her what had happened to Anthony. Then:

"Are you sure it's him?"

"Don't you recognize him?" she said, arching her eyebrows, incredulous and mocking.

And, at full speed, she replayed that extraordinary archive of Anthony's nudity. Beside him, E. Blaye looked short and drab. Her skin seemed to be made of wax, her hair of wool. She smiled tightly, lips pressed together, while Anthony seemed to take every opportunity to exhibit his teeth, whiter and more regular than René remembered.

"René doesn't recognize our Anthony," said Madame Mour indulgently, turning toward Anthony's brother, who'd just come in.

The Mour brother grunted, amused. He glanced vaguely at the screen, gave René a slap on the back. Then Madame Mour turned off the computer, explaining that the Mour father would be home any minute, and there was no way he...

"He can't stand this, God knows why," said Madame Mour.

She gave a dry little laugh. She asked René what was so terrible about it. René was trembling all over. He couldn't come up with an answer. Madame Mour shook her head and made an indignant face.

"Here we are, finally digging out from our troubles, and my husband wants to quibble about the methods. Anthony's a success, someone was willing to take him in, he helps out his parents, it's only natural. Isn't that natural? Wouldn't you follow a woman, any woman, René, to rescue your mother from hardship?"

"Help me," René murmured.

"Help you?"

"I'm for sale, same as Anthony. Find someone who wants to buy me. Please."

Madame Mour sat back, crossed her arms. She studied René, reflecting. Snug in a new pair of pants, her long legs shifted gently from one side of the chair to the other.

"It won't be easy, my little René," she said. "But I'll try."

Leaving the Mours' farm to head homeward again, René's excitement almost kept him from noticing the Mour father coming and going from the pickup truck to the barn, transporting all sorts of tools and bags with stolid determination, rubber boots on his feet, and wearing a broad hat that left René, whose heart was swelling with joyful hope, half expecting to see the Mour father leap onto his horse and gallop off toward adventures without end.

René broke into a laugh. How he loved the Mours, all four of them, even Anthony's brother, without whom Anthony's grace would stand out less brilliantly—how he loved the Mours, how he loved, he repeated to himself, every good little family!

His own seemed no less worthy of affection that evening, when he realized he'd soon be telling them goodbye. And with this, the squirming, tangled mass of neglected children, the caustic, gloomy, indolent presence of his mother, even the tyrannical imposition of food to be eaten by him and him alone (some dish of noodles glistening with butter, veritably bellowing at him from the other end of the table), none of it could get to him now, nothing could enrage or defeat him. From time to time the memory of a naked Anthony raced through his mind, gilded, exultant, displaying his teeth (whitened?), his legs spread wide in a virile stance, index finger upraised before his lips (plumped with silicone?), and nose (reshaped, slenderized?), as if mischievously swearing the viewer to secrecy, and then, dizzied, he wondered if that really was Anthony Mour, if Anthony's new existence could one day be his, René's, his physique duly amended, if, in short, anything was possible, even his own acquisition by... not by E. Blaye, but... but why shouldn't she have two boys around her to... to do what? René's head was gently swimming. To serve her, to show her off at her best, to ease her sorrows, to love her deeply?

"I can do anything," murmured René, gripped by an uneasy vainglory, a tremulous joy.

He'd always known he could make a gift of himself. Assuming someone would take him, assuming someone was eager to have him, him, a colorless boy named René, he could subjugate himself to the will of anyone at all. Little matter if he was purchased or picked up for free. Either way, for him, it would mean making a gift of himself. But...

What had he seen, that cruel night the previous summer, in the cold gaze of the man who, as he carelessly strolled down the hill between two fields of corn, grudgingly informed him that he was his father? What had he seen, if not, more excruciating than hostility, an irreparable shame? And then a glacial dismissiveness, a scornful "keep your distance," instantly and expressly aimed at that disappointing, insignificant boy, René, by this stranger who, René could clearly see, no one could possibly consider a catch? Before that evening, René still believed he had only to offer himself with conviction, and he would be taken—but if no one ever sees you, where do you find the courage to tell the world you're there, open and new, just waiting to be snatched up? If no one ever even sees you?

René walked down the highway, cut across furniture-store parking lots and car dealerships, stepped over the railroad tracks, went on through abandoned depots with graffiti-sprayed walls, his pace eager and brisk. Reaching the start of the Way of the Cross in the nearby pilgrimage town, he wiped the sweat from his face and set off uphill. He paused at the first station to kneel and mumble he didn't quite know what. A woman was already there, and René nudged her a little to one side.

"Well, really!" she huffed.

She shot René a glance. Then she hurried to her feet and somewhat stiffly raced off toward the next stop, further uphill. Noting her bare feet, René took off his old shoes and stuffed one into each pocket. He joined his hesitant hands.

"Let me be bought, bought, bought."

The sun shone through the unstirring boughs of the tall ash trees and fell in lacy patches onto the road, which was littered with crumpled papers that René carefully sidestepped. He was surprised to find the dusty asphalt so cool against his soles, struck by the desert-like, timeworn stillness of this place of devotion. "Bought, bought," sang the half-broken concrete figures beneath each little shelter, in an echo. "Let me be bought, and I promise..."

"I won't be choosy," René whispered fervently. "I'll go with the first person who wants me."

Had he the right not to suffer, he who was asking so much? He continued his climb, deliberately treading on anything that showed some sign of sharpness. At the very top, he met up with the barefoot woman again, and she eyed him in fear and defiance as she knelt on the steps before the enormous, severe, gilt-covered statue of Anthony Mour amid his disciples.

René dropped to his knees alongside her, breathless, his feet smarting, but stunned, almost blinded, by what he'd just seen. Finally he found the courage to look up again, hesitant and awed. And saw... Glorious, Anthony Mour looked benevolently down at him, still nude, apart from the customary strip of cloth vaguely knotted around his slim hips. René immediately lowered his eyes. Flashes of violent, slashing light shot through his skull. A sort of shame turned his face crimson. Anthony Mour saw this, and he knew what naïve hope had brought René to this place, alone beside the believer who was now sitting on a step, knees apart, trying to cram her fat feet into the shoes she'd pulled from her shopping bag, puffing and grumbling—Anthony Mour saw it all, he who never had to pray to be desired. Perhaps Anthony Mour was about to speak, gently mock him, pity him. Or tell him, perhaps, that his chances, or his hopes... If he could only summon the strength to look up one last time, would he not find that one of the disciples bore René's face, beneath the gilding? Idiotic, ugly, but wholeheartedly faithful René's face?

He sensed a change at the Mours' farm even before he got there, as if all around it the warm air were trembling with excitement. The big white farmyard was empty—no chickens, no dogs, only a truck bearing the name and particulars of a masonry business. Anthony's brother was standing near the door, his back to the wall. He clutched René's arm as he passed, his hand adorned by two rings, a tiny watch set into each.

"My father took off," he said unemotionally.

Thinking he'd heard in this a thinly veiled threat whose motivation and nature escaped him, René said nothing. He froze in place, transparent.

"He killed all the animals before he left," the brother went on.

"The dogs too?"

"All of them, I said. He did it in the barn. You'll have to deal with it."

René didn't move, so the brother added, with a sly, cocky smirk:

"My mother said so. She said, 'Let René deal with it.'"

He licked his greedy lips and let out a little laugh, not untinged, René was heartened to notice, by distress. And as he crossed the forlorn farmyard, so heavy with that deathly silence he'd mistaken for a breathless pause heralding some new beginning, René could feel Anthony's brother's fixed stare tickling his back, and he had the unsettling sense that the Mour brother had fallen into a bleak, nameless unhappiness, and didn't even know it. But why? And what was the point? Would René not have taken fervid delight in being the brother of Anthony Mour and the son of Madame Mour, who could imbue the gesture of brushing a lock of hair from her cheek with an awareness of herself and her dignity that, even in her moments of greatest triumph (a new marriage, money coming in) or greatest pleasure, René's mother had never managed to summon?

Heading toward the barn, René quaked with contempt for Anthony's brother. One man was as good as another, he knew. Who could possibly think the Mour father had no equal? One man went away, soon replaced by another just like him, and the mother went on unchanged.

He spent much of the afternoon behind the barn, burying the four fine, powerful dogs that filled the Mour father with unconcealed vanity. He'd killed them cleanly, with one rifle shot apiece. As for the chickens, their throats slit, René stuffed them into a garbage bag to take home with him.

When he finally, timidly entered the kitchen, it was with a sense that his place in the Mour's home had subtly changed. He even conceived the wild idea that with the money sent her by Anthony, Madame Mour might not be averse to buying René, since…What other boy around here…But if every boy in the region was for sale, what hope was there for René? Tormented, he silently approached the little table where Madame Mour sat glued to her computer, her bare legs crossed to one side, a red velvet slipper hanging from the end of one foot. The kitchen was in complete disarray. Two workmen wearing nothing but shorts were taking out the sink, a third prying off the old tiles. Catching sight of the fourth, who was busy sanding a wall, René quickly looked away, convinced that this man was his father.

He gently touched Madame Mour's shoulder.

"Oh, it's you, René...Look at you, what a mess," she murmured wearily.

He winced. It hadn't occurred to him that his hands were red with the blood of the chickens and dogs. Madame Mour's own cheeks were mottled and haggard, her eyes drowning in sorrow. On the computer screen, an animated image showed Anthony running through a field of astonishingly green grass. Still tall, lithe, and nude, his smile never faded as he bounded with pure, vigorous strides through ever new spaces, infinite, filled with fluorescent verdure. René glanced behind him. Now his father was surreptitiously eyeing the screen. Anger welled up in René.

"What's happening to you?" he whispered.

"You know...He's gone...My husband."

Madame Mour's lips were trembling.

"It was the money from Anthony. He didn't want any part of it, in his house or his life."

"That's nothing to be sad about," said René, furious. "Come on now, that's nothing to be sad about."

"What can you possibly know about it, my poor René?" said Madame Mour after a pause.

She froze Anthony's picture, enlarged it for a clearer view of his body and face, his features quivering in the embrace of an unutterable happiness, then turned away from the computer, leaving Anthony's nudity and elation displayed on the screen, consoling and breathtaking.

René noticed that his father was now staring openly at

the screen. All at once his rage fell away. He felt pointless, sterile, laughable. Realizing that his father hadn't recognized him, hadn't even noticed him, he stopped trying to keep his back turned.

"René, I've found someone for you," said Madame Mour.

Her slipper fell to the ground. René picked it up and slid it over Madame Mour's foot, while behind him someone snickered.

And two days later René found himself by the side of the highway, waiting. With his worn little suitcase nearby in the grass, he peered into the gold and white distance beyond the dusty ribbon of concrete, untraveled at this early hour. The towering cornstalks rustled cheerily all around him. René answered them with joyous, knowing little laughs. How delicious was his mother's surprise on learning he'd been singled out, chosen, picked—and how deep her humiliation, surely, that it was Madame Mour who'd managed to sell René, and not her, his own mother.

He was sweating with eagerness. His chest itched where he'd carefully shaved himself to imitate smooth-skinned Anthony. And the mirror had told him... almost told him... that he was becoming... Could it be?

All alone, René flexed his muscles. Oh, yes, less ugly, less skinny, less...

On the horizon, the tiny dot of a car was growing larger. Suddenly there it was, stopped in front of René, even more luxurious than the one E. Blaye had driven out to pick up Anthony Mour.

René opened the trunk, gaily tossed his shameful suitcase inside.

He sat down in the front seat: as the car silently pulled away, he finally found the courage to turn his head and see who was holding the wheel.

And a horrified cry rose to his lips, and he pressed them violently together. Nothing escaped but a moan, a submissive whimper of dread and regret.

BRULARD'S DAY

So Brulard, Eve Brulard, slipped out of the Hotel Bellerive at the earliest possible hour, as if she knew with precision and certainty which way to set off.

She didn't. So utterly didn't she know that her right leg seemed intent on opposing her left leg's decision to head toward the lake, and she stood walking in place for a few seconds before the veranda, shocked by the damp cold but still too stiff and sleepy to bother turning up the collar of her light jacket, and also vaguely telling herself, scarcely emerged from a dream: first thing this morning, if the money has come, I'll go buy a coat. Then it occurred to her that any step she took to feel a tiny bit less cold in her jacket, turning up the collar or tugging down the sleeves, would misleadingly assure the forces guiding her luck that this little jacket was perfectly sufficient—and that, consequently, there was no need for the money. Better to act as though she didn't even have a jacket to protect her.

It was so much colder here than where Brulard had come from.

It's so much colder, she thought, and she gave a clenched little smile to the night clerk she could see through the glass door, preparing to make way for his daytime colleague, whose skeptical, scrutinizing gaze she studiously avoided whenever she passed by the front desk, her head high. From the start, she'd sensed that he thought her neither radiant nor carefree, despite all her efforts to seem just that. And so she'd taken to leaving her room at daybreak, heaving herself out of bed with difficulty and a dazed misery that filled her entire ill-rested body, so that she could breezily appear before the night clerk and exchange a few words on the color of the lake and the fog, painfully aware of the hurried, imprecise work she'd done on her face with foundation, tinted powder, and a shimmering lipstick up in her room, but hoping the night clerk would once again fail to see that she was still wearing the same black clothes as before, now a little shiny, and that her face, aspiring to a certain impersonal, indisputable harmoniousness with the help of the makeup, was in fact rumpled by an all-consuming exhaustion.

And so what if he did? Brulard asked herself out on the icy sidewalk, so what if the receptionist did notice that... that what? She didn't want to seem disreputable. She wanted people to think well of the woman she was, she wanted people to think her prosperous enough to pay for a few nights in a moderately luxurious hotel without troubling herself over it, she wanted to seem unique, casual, and proud. No one here had recognized Brulard. Neither the day clerk's bored dubiousness nor the night clerk's placid indifference suggested that they found Brulard's face in any way familiar.

She told herself none of that mattered to her. Standing between the veranda and the road, shivering but, numbed as she was by fatigue, by a fatigue verging on stupor, not entirely aware that it really was her feeling cold, and not a cardboard cutout of her set up outside the hotel to publicize an exclusive engagement (but never had her unassuming fame propelled her to any such level of visibility, and now it never would), she limply decided to head for the lake. She stamped the ground to warm her feet, shod in brown tassel loafers. That she'd been reduced to wearing such shoes tormented and astonished her at the same time.

She sensed a presence above her, and, raising her eyes to the window of her second-floor room, she found Eve Brulard staring down at her with concern and benevolence, her elbows on the sill. The Eve Brulard at the window was at most twenty years old. What did she have to be concerned about? Irritated and stern, Brulard hissed through her teeth, tss tss, and, with a little cry of terror or derision, a strident plaint that drilled into Brulard's eardrums, the young Eve Brulard evaporated into the fog that had rolled in from the lake. Thank goodness, she thought, no one but her ever heard the blood-curdling cries emitted by this shrieking snake-woman, who nevertheless always seemed to appear in a context of steadfast understanding and solicitude. Why, then, this look of concern on Eve's youthful face, since Brulard had, in spite of everything, more reasons to rejoice than to worry? And was it not increasingly wearying to find the young woman she'd once been now showing up in all manner of circumstances and anywhere at all, anytime, never particularly wished for by Brulard, who never received from her any clear revelation on any subject whatever, who couldn't even escape her by closing her eyes, who was forced to accept this friend's sporadic company as one mutely endures a mysterious threat, as one passively accepts a message of regrets, of good wishes, of condolence? Brulard wished it would stop. Some days she encountered that figure so often that she forgot that her own face had changed, and, happening onto a mirror, momentarily wondered: who is that no-longer-very-young woman, and what's she doing in my light?

She circled around the hotel and immediately found herself on the lakeshore. The water was gray that morning, and a thick fog hid the houses on the other side, giving Brulard, numb with fatigue, the disturbing feeling of an endless dawn, a suspended daybreak that would never stop spreading its cottony mists over a leaden lake for the sole purpose of wearing down her vital forces.

Because it was still far too early to seek some sort of escape. Where was there to go, what to do? Not even the cafés were open at this hour. As for the bank, the moment when Brulard could push open the double glazed doors, forcing herself to abandon all hope and pasting a stern, incensed look on her face, that moment still seemed so remote that she refused even to think about it, fearing her thoughts' dizzying plunge into boredom, and the memory of all the boredom past, and all the wasted hours.

Nevertheless, she had more reasons to rejoice than to... But how simply to get through these few days of solitude by the lake, Brulard couldn't imagine.

She walked slowly, feeling the tassels on her shoes jump against the fine leather. Those shoes were an innocent presage of some subtly morbid change in her way of seeing things, for, in all her sometimes tangled and disappointing life, would she ever, at any time, have bought loafers of her own volition? Before last Saturday, when, alighting from the train, she saw lingering patches of muddy snow on the platform, realized she couldn't stay here with only sandals to wear, entered the first shoe store she came to, and picked out these medium-heel slip-ons, before that April Saturday when she had, in a sense, fled her own house (as Brulard said to herself, not that she'd actually had to flee, not that anyone would have tried to hold her back or even thought of doing so, much less believed holding her back to be possible or desirable), before that Saturday her violent hatred of such shoes, so unmistakably designed for comfort, ease of mobility, and charitable deeds, was like a reflexive surge of free will in the teeth of the dictates of respectable taste. A Catholic lady's shoes, thought Brulard, bewildered that she'd found it necessary, as punishment for deserting Lulu, to disguise herself in this way. But maybe that's not what it was. Maybe she herself was becoming...

Brulard felt the mountain behind her, watching. Still invisible, cloud-draped, the mountain sloped down to the lake. No matter which way she turned, Brulard felt the mountain nearby, and she sensed that this austere presence was only one of the many incarnations chosen by her mother, dead not long before, to weigh on Brulard's conscience. But, oh, being watched didn't scare her. She was on her way, resolutely, toward a new happiness.

But, Brulard wondered, why was it so hard, now that she really was alone, to feel that unplanned isolation in all its plenitude and rarity, and to enjoy it in some way, rather than, as she caught herself doing at this very moment, turning her head to avoid the eye of the young Eve Brulard, who now sat on a bench facing the lake, staring at her loafers, wearing an extravagant pink chiffon dress that clearly displayed her pointed, youthful breasts, her little brown shoulders, her narrow, curved pelvis? And rather than, once she'd done that, immediately looking down so as not to glimpse the snow-covered mass of the mountain behind the clouds, now gradually unfurling, mutating into a sort of gauze not unlike the pink fabric of the dress that...?

Better, with the mountain so hostile and so indiscreet, to fix her gaze on the lake's tranquil waters, or the bench, now rid of the exhausting presence of the beauteous Eve Brulard, whose eagle eye had not missed those tasseled shoes—and then, on her smooth face, was that the shadow of a surge of pity? Of a reproach, tinged by compassion and alarm?

Brulard sat on the bench, her lids heavy. She rested one cheek on her shoulder and wrapped her arms around her knees. She felt the cold numbing her, drawing her toward sleep, toward surrender. She pictured herself in the place of Eve Brulard, possessed of all the self-assurance, the litheness, the punctilious critical sensibility of a twenty-year-old, and tried to see herself through those eyes—leaving the loafers aside, just this once. What did you see when you looked at Brulard? A slight, mild woman with a dark complexion, short black hair, an unsuitable, slightly shiny jacket and trousers, large, timid, obstinate eyes, and on her lips a faint quivering bitterness, increasingly difficult to transmute into joyous surprise? Or some vast, looming personage of ambiguous sex, a fine face, hard and square, a strong jaw hungry for conquest and success? Brulard had no doubt that at times she'd been exactly that, magnified by ambition and self-confidence even more than by her high heels, next to which the modest loafers looked like two runts shrunken into their own virtue, by her thick mane of bleached, champagne-blonde hair, carefully styled to halo her head, by the proud bearing of her shoulders, of her ramrod-straight neck. Which of those two Brulards did you see at this moment? And which was the one who was loved, or preferred? The tall, blonde, almost famous Brulard, or the Brulard of today, slighter, but whose expression, she could see in her every reflection, was that of a grave, discreet ecstasy, of passion without illusions, unbowed even if battered? Was this second one not inevitably the favorite? Of those two possible versions of Eve Brulard between forty and fifty years of age? By the grace of a sincerity that she herself found mysterious (for what her true current face had to do with her she had no idea, and this ignorance left her pensive, perplexed), but which that artificial ambitious blondness and that chin held a little too high professed less convincingly?

Brulard had a secret soft spot in her heart for the blonde, hungry Brulard, even if that one had misjudged the best way to go about succeeding, even though she'd given far too much of herself for very middling results. Brulard even felt a certain disdain for the simple, natural woman she seemed so quickly to have become, the very one who, to punish herself for racing toward a shining new future, now almost in sight, had snatched up the first pair of loafers she laid eyes on. She knew that no such need for self-mortification would ever have entered the mind of the ravishing Brulard of old, and certainly not for a reason like this, for behaving in a way that might bring something remarkable into her life, even if it came at the expense of great sorrow.

But, for the moment, how tired she was.

Day had now fully broken, giving the lake that cobalt blue tint that had intimidated Brulard when she first stepped off the train, a perfectly and literally honest blue that she had immediately seen as the emblem of this entire adventure. May what I'm now making my way toward, she'd said to herself, be just as…

How tired she was.

Eyes half-closed, she gave a start. A warm, dry snout had brushed against her limply hanging hand. An ugly little dog with a drab coat was clasping a crumpled piece of paper between its teeth. Brulard smiled. It was the homeliest, most pathetic-looking dog she'd ever seen. She reached out to give it a cautious caress. The dog licked her fingers, the paper fell to the ground, and Brulard, having first pretended not to notice, quickly picked it up, faintly stunned. It was just what she thought she'd seen in that dog's mouth—the word *Hassler*. She felt herself blushing stupidly. A jogger came into view, and Brulard, assuming he was the dog's owner, gently pushed the animal his way with the tip of her shoe. The athlete sped past at a panting little trot in his luxurious white and gold outfit, never glancing toward the bench. Puffs of flatulence drifted along in his wake.

Brulard buried her head in her hands. She'd read that word *Hassler* on the paper—could it be? Was this a portent of good things to come? Or a questionable gift from the mountain that Brulard could no longer pretend not to see, now that the new day was extracting it from the fog, at once behind Brulard's back and in front of her, almost up to the opposite shore—still snow-covered in its upper reaches, now unable to hide its likeness, in physiognomy and expression, to Brulard's late mother, or rather old mother Brulard, as she was called in her village, off in the province of Berry, like a failed avatar or a ridiculous disguise? It was her, Brulard's mother, impossible to catch in the act, watching and mutely disapproving of Brulard for the rest of time. Here a mountain, there a footpath or a hill—everywhere, in fact.

Who cares? Brulard asked herself.

Had she fallen asleep? A large cold sun was flooding her bench. A well-to-do crowd strolled along the promenade, lined leather boots, pastel down coats, a whole childish winter-sport elegance that demoralized Brulard, who, in her black clothes, seemed some sort of evil fairy alighted here to darken the children's festivities. Had she fallen asleep? It was almost eleven. She'd missed the opening of the bank, and now she'd have to hurry to be there before noon. She stood up, then gingerly sat down again, shaken.

Had she been recognized?

Her head was spinning with impatience and apprehension. Who here knew of her private affinity with the mountain? A smile crossed her lips as she imagined the stunned dismay on these faces, so blessed by sunshine and money, if she told them just who that mountain was (and what vulgarity would they not immediately find in the presence of an "old mother Brulard" deep inside their costly mountain), and yet, thought Brulard, there was one thing she didn't know: whether, for each of these vacationers, a mother Brulard of their own, named by each in their own secret way, might have adopted that mountain's form and appearance, spying, judging, thinking herself alone, and every one of them, like Brulard, thinking her alone and unique.

It was nearing noon when Brulard returned to her hotel. Disappointment had granted her a glorious, go-for-broke daring. She took out her checkbook and, smiling boldly and broadly with all her hard-won technique, regretting as she strode toward the desk that she'd lacked this foolhardy courage a little while before, and hadn't bought that much-needed coat on leaving the bank, she rested her elbows on the counter directly in front of the clerk. Thrusting forward her cold, shining, pinkened face, she exclaimed:

"Hello! I'd like to pay for the three days I've been here."

All the while thinking to herself, trembling, oddly excited: the check's going to bounce.

She slid the paper she'd taken from the dog—a pale yellow sheet, smoothed out by her own hand—toward the unsmiling clerk.

"They're showing a film I act in at the Rio...This one here... *The Death of Claire Hassler.*"

Her smile widened still further, her jaw aching vaguely. How vicious must the shock of a letdown be to send you tumbling from hope into despair? She could feel herself teetering, and that unsteadiness energized her, cleansed her of her weakness.

"This one here, see?...That's right, I'm in it."

"Oh, that. I've seen it," said the employee.

He examined Brulard's check more closely than was polite. He was a young blond man, pale and cold, who, from the first day, Brulard thought, treated her as if awaiting the moment when he would at long last see through her, patient, sure it would come.

"Did you like it?" asked Brulard, slightly breathless.

The young man wouldn't look her in the eye. He let a few seconds go by, with Brulard's face, glowing in artificial eagerness, a little too close to his, and then he let it drop:

"I don't know. I wouldn't have thought it was you."

"Who?"

"The woman whose brain gets...tinkered with," he said delicately. "In the movie. I don't recognize you."

"That's not me," Brulard warmly cried out, suddenly so eager to win a little consideration from this boy that she shook her head and gave a chummy little laugh. "I play the other one, the heroine's sister. You know, the one who's so merry and bold."

But he had no memory of that character, apart, he observed to Brulard in an irritable voice, from a yellow scarf that came loose and got stuck in a car door.

"Yes, that's right," Brulard murmured.

And then, considering the subject closed, the young man turned away. Speechless, wondering in a fierce fit of panic how on earth she could fill up the rest of her day, Brulard pulled her tremulous, weary face back toward herself, wistfully withdrawing it from the cold sphere created all around the young man by his indifference, his distant indolence. She reflexively touched her cheeks, her forehead—and so, without meaning to, evidently summoned up the meddlesome young Eve Brulard, who abruptly took the employee's place behind the counter, making conventional obscene gestures at Brulard, still half clad in her translucent pink dress, now rumpled and torn. Never before had Brulard seen her show the least sign of spite, or at least of sarcasm and vulgarity. Afraid, she thrust out her fingers, and the girl disappeared with an overdone snort of derision. The boy had turned around again—had Brulard's fingers unwittingly touched him, as if to give him a teasing little slap, a flirtatious flick? She thought they very possibly had, though she couldn't be certain. She turned beet red, blurted out:

"Excuse me!"

He shot her a brief glance, conscientiously drained of all expression, but should she go on believing that no one but her could make out the hideous screeches of that half-naked girl in the chiffon dress? That girl who, no doubt—but Brulard had absolutely no desire to make sure, convinced that Eve was only waiting for her to look up to start shrieking again—was now flitting this way and that around the big crystal chandelier? Brulard herself could so clearly hear the pink fabric rustling overhead, and the mocking little sounds the girl's mouth made for her benefit, but how was she to know? Suppose that girl was deliberately provoking the young clerk, so that she, Brulard…

A tongue vigorously licked her hand, and there was that awful brown dog again, with the squashed nose and the slightly overlong ears, the unlikely crossbreed she'd encountered a little earlier, by the lakeside. Good-hearted and peaceable, it looked at Brulard with disinterested affection. It was dirty, repugnant.

"What's that?" the employee grumbled from behind the counter.

"Oh, he's with me," said Jimmy's voice.

"Wait, you have a dog now?" said Brulard with a stunned laugh, a yelp of pained incredulity.

Even more aghast, almost, to learn that this was Jimmy's dog than she was to see Jimmy here in this hotel, so distant did that Saturday now seem, so like something from an entirely different age of their lives, that previous Saturday, when the idea of running away and the actual running away had taken shape in the space of two short hours, the hotel and the lake and the bank decided on with only a brief conversation, whispered and breathless, from cellphone to cellphone—and now Brulard, engulfed in melancholy, was regretting that that phone call lay behind her, that those quivering, conspiratorial minutes, full of something like ardent youth, were now in the past.

Suddenly, Jimmy was here, and with that how could Brulard not find her sense of impetuousness absurd?

"Where's Lulu?" asked Brulard, wearily.

"On holiday with the Alphonses," Jimmy quickly replied.

She scowled in distaste and surprise. She patted the dog's head, hoping Jimmy might tell her something more about the animal, but her husband said nothing. In his pale eye, now fixed on her, she thought she made out a tinge of pity that filled her with alarm. Was it not in fact Jimmy who deserved a pitying gaze? Was it not him who'd been abandoned without one word of warning, not for fear of some anguished reaction, but in anticipation of the staggering boredom that his voice and his grim, gentle face always unleashed when he tried to prevail, to explain himself, to defend himself? Hey, Jimmy, there's nothing to explain, Brulard would simply have said, no more than you can convince someone they're loved. Hey, Jimmy, Brulard would have said, irritated, nobody can do that, can they? Instead of which, swept along by a passion, an inner lyricism she hadn't felt for a very long time, she'd said nothing, and her leaving was like an escape, and the murmurs into the telephone like the whispers of two cautious accomplices, although there was nothing they had to protect themselves from, nor, truth be told, anything to protect.

And now Jimmy was here, and his mere presence made Brulard's amorous adventures ridiculous, all the more implacably in that Jimmy was looking exceptionally sunny, and unexpectedly elegant (and just how, Brulard snickered to herself, had he paid for those pants and that leather jacket?), his unjustified but wholly convincing air of prosperity underscored by the contrast with the dog's shabbiness, as if, out of nothing other than snobbery, Jimmy thought himself far too fine to associate with a handsome beast.

Brulard felt small and pointless. She recalled that the money hadn't been deposited into her account, that she'd had in fact no word at all, despite all she'd been promised. Briefly pushed to one side, her exhaustion came flooding back. She felt a little vein throbbing in one eyelid.

"So, Jimmy, you got yourself this dog to replace me?" she said with a forced laugh.

"He was following me, and I adopted him because I thought he was you," Jimmy said gravely.

"That dog, me?"

"I thought he was you. Granted, I might have been mistaken."

Brulard's telephone rang in her pocket. She couldn't hold back a dry sob: she'd been waiting so long for this. She gently pressed the telephone to her ear, sidling away from Jimmy. At first, no one answered her meekly whispered "Hello." Only a heavy silence.

"You've had your fun," growled a man's voice unknown to Brulard, so thrumming with malice that she frantically switched off the phone and thrust it deep into her pocket.

She raised two fingers to her lips. Help, help, she moaned. But she must not have made a sound, because Jimmy gave her a little wave from across the lobby, suddenly all smiles. Behind his counter, the employee was looking at Jimmy with a respectful benevolence he'd never shown Brulard, far from it. Who are my friends? Brulard asked herself. Who's watching over me? Whose sympathy... A piercing cry echoed in her head, though, to Brulard's great relief, the young Eve

Brulard was nowhere to be seen, and in a fit of wounded, pathetic pride she answered Jimmy's smile with a similarly easy smile, decorous, distinguished. She was terrified. *You've had your fun*—but how could anyone, how could a humble soul generally and in every way doing the best she could, arouse so much hatred? And could it truly be said that she'd ever in her life actually had fun?

Jimmy's dog ran toward her, leapt up, dampened her cheek with a hearty lick. For the few seconds that the dog's eyes were level with Brulard's, she had the brutal feeling that she could see her own anxious soul reflected or submerged deep inside them. The dark mirror of the dog's pupils seemed to be showing her not her own miniaturized face but something else, unexpected, inexplicable—as if, Brulard told herself at a loss, her appearance had suddenly changed beyond all recognition, or as if the dog's incomprehensible black eye were reflecting Brulard's true, secret being, of which she herself had no notion, which she couldn't describe, even on finding it thus revealed in the gaze of that pitiful creature.

"I brought you some things," said Jimmy, suddenly close enough to brush against her.

And he went on, very quietly, his chin wrinkling up, his hairless, satiny face suddenly contorted:

"Oh, why did you go away? Tell me why?"

A moment later he got hold of himself. He stood up straight, twisted his mouth into a self-deprecating little grin. Good old Jimmy, thought Brulard gratefully, brave, thoughtful Jimmy. Unless what brought Jimmy here was something very different from what she assumed (her husband's slightly fussy and excessive thoughtfulness). Was there not once again a sort of free-floating pity in the surreptitious glances he cast at her, at her body, her hair? She felt a surge of anger and fear. But, smiling, she gently shook her head. What's happened? Who is my friend, my guardian? How I wish I could lie down for a few minutes, Brulard thought. To her deep chagrin, she felt an embittered wariness toward Jimmy taking root in her.

"Who was that on the phone?" he asked.

"I think... it's none of your business," Brulard mumbled.

With difficulty, she added:

"The fact is, I have no idea."

They stood face to face, tense and still, but knowing each other so well in adversity that a sort of weariness fell over Brulard, and she told herself she'd been through all this before, in different circumstances.

"Needless to say, Lulu stays with me," said Jimmy in a hard voice.

He went on:

"Forever, no matter what."

"Forever?"

And Brulard could feel the smile on her frozen face, her exquisite, imperceptibly mocking smile, at which Jimmy would certainly not take offense, for he knew her as well as she knew him, and he knew that the more insulting, painful, and unjust was her meaning, the more overt and delicious Brulard's smile would be, and the more carefree her voice.

"I'll come and see Lulu whenever I can," she nevertheless said, in a tone so sharp and unbridled that a sort of alarm, an unease softened Jimmy's intractable gaze, as she thought to herself: he doesn't know how terribly I need to sleep, everything's different when you wake up, even Eve Brulard finds it hard to pursue me when I'm well rested.

She gave Jimmy a gentle cuff on the chin. He scowled. Defying him, but purring, wheedling, she asked:

"How did you find out where I was? Who told you? Oh, never mind, I don't want to know."

Lulu's pale adolescent face suddenly drifted into Brulard's memory, replacing the face that had occupied her every thought since the previous Saturday, that broad, serious face, thoughtful and worn, whose solicitous gravity Brulard's unquiet mind ceaselessly summoned up, and each time she came back from the bank she reassured herself a little with the memory of that dignity, of that loyalty, just as she did when, every evening before slipping into the hotel's narrow bed, she found herself forced to acknowledge that another day had gone by with no phone call—Lulu's sweet face, round-cheeked, confident, and tender, which Brulard hadn't seen one last time before she went away, Lulu having spent all that Saturday at a friend's, and would she have left had Lulu's eyes been upon her, would she have raced off toward an exciting new life? Yes, yes, Brulard told herself, paralyzed by melancholy, she most certainly would have, for can you forego the possibility of a windfall of fate, of a miraculous down payment on freedom from doubt and monotony? Who would willingly spurn such a grace bestowed without explanation, with no need for thanks or gratitude? Who?—except, in her day, old mother Brulard, whose immortality in the form of a stern mountain was perhaps her only reward for her many renunciations.

Brulard's drifting thoughts came and went around Lulu. She felt a dribble of saliva on her chin and realized she was drooling. She wiped her face with the back of her hand, thinking: It's the exhaustion. If I could only…Who's stopping me?

But was it even imaginable that Jimmy would let her sleep?

He was talking with the clerk. Eyelids pinched with exhaustion, she let her gaze linger on Jimmy's slender back, oddly youthful in that bottle-green, scraped leather jacket—which was strange, she thought, because she'd seen it as burgundy just a short while before, and she'd thought: is burgundy a tolerable color for an article of clothing, and now she found it to be, or saw it as, the same conscientious green as the hotel's armchairs, which several guests just out of the dining room were approaching, preparing to drop heavily into them, and now they were sitting there, exhaling deeply, murmuring gravely, waiting for the sun to warm the shores of the lake, as if they had a time without limit before them, a distended, opulent time. How wonderful it will be, Brulard thought, to be old. Oh, how wonderful it would be to be rich.

She backed very discreetly toward the elevator, eyes trained on Jimmy. He was bantering with the clerk, swaying his hips and slightly raising his shoulders, and Brulard told herself she would slip away to her room, lock herself in, and sleep till early afternoon. For all she knew Jimmy would be gone when she woke, and perhaps she would even have forgotten his coming, perhaps even, in an abrupt return of mystery and good luck, she might find, languishing in one of those armchairs, the man for the love of whom she was here, alone and needy under the watch of the hated mountain.

Jimmy's dog barked after her. That filthy animal's onto me, Brulard thought. Supple, feline, Jimmy immediately glided across the lobby to her side.

"There's only one free room," he said, his brow anxious.

"You're not going to…"

"Why not?"

She gave a feverish, incredulous little laugh.

"As far as I'm concerned, I'm on vacation," Jimmy said, with a strangely pleased air.

Sliding airily over the wooden floor, as if letting himself be wafted along unawares, he arrived at the side of the silent, apathetic Swiss couple in the armchairs. He tossed the cinema program that Brulard had left at the counter onto the woman's thighs. In his low, cajoling voice, she heard him intoning:

"There…That's Eve Brulard, look…She's my wife, she has a part in this film. It's a…wonderful film. I recommend…"

She thought she could also hear him telling them of a lemon-yellow scarf that stayed stuck in a car door as it started off.

"What about your wife? Inside the car, or out?" the man asked, bending down to hear better.

Jimmy burst into a charming laugh. Suddenly alarmed, the dog began to bark. Jimmy didn't seem to notice, and

Brulard observed that the clerk, so brusque with her, so clearly distressed to be mixed up with her in anything slightly strange or ridiculous, scarcely glanced up at the dog, before, with an understanding, fraternal little smile, going back to his work.

"I've never worn a scarf in my life," Brulard heard, as she tentatively wandered past the Swiss couple, both of them still young and childishly blond and giving her an indifferent, dubious glance, as if, thought Brulard, they weren't entirely convinced she was there.

"Yes, you did, you did—and a yellow scarf, furthermore," the man insisted. "That day, you tied a yellow scarf around your neck."

"A wonderful, wonderful film," Jimmy said again, ingratiating and obsequious, with a certain lively, quick-witted grace.

But, wondered Brulard, what did he really want from these people? Or did he not want anything from them at all, but wanted only to keep her from leaving, by creating a diversion from her distress, from her sorrow—for surely one glance at Brulard's face had shown him she hadn't found that state of joy and superiority without which her flight had no purpose?

A sort of gauzy veil imprisoned Brulard's head as she walked through the flag-draped streets, Jimmy on her right, holding her elbow so delicately that at first she didn't feel it, and when she did finally take note of that discreet support, the unpleasantness of having to express anything at all dispensed her from stepping away from Jimmy. Was he desperately wanting to touch her before he never had the chance again? Or was this a way of holding her captive, of pretending that, so gently herded, she'd allow herself to be led, unresisting, to the train, to the house?

Those days are over, she wanted to tell him, my life's different now, and I'm so far away from you that... But she feared that the slightest word might shatter her skull.

The dog trotted along obediently on her left. Framed by Jimmy and his hideous dog, Brulard felt pathetic, ridiculous. A wave of pity and anger welled up inside her. A vague indignation struggled to poke through her fogged thoughts, born, she knew well, of a painful awareness that she was not going to be left alone.

"Lovely town," Jimmy was saying. "Ah, how nice."

And then, whispering a still-stunned desolation into her ear:

"Why did you go away? Why?"

Brulard looked, unseeing, at the pale yellow and almond green facades, the luxurious shop windows, the souvenir stores with awnings weighed down by multiple cowbells, a whole landscape that she now knew so well, having paced through it each day since she came here, and toward which she had come to feel only resentment. Those same little flower-decked bridges straddling the canals, those same cobblestone streets, overlooked by those same charming balconies that Jimmy was now stopping to admire, his chin raised and his hand pressed visor-like to his forehead, letting out half stifled gasps of pleasure, had seen her morning after morning, fighting back a mounting despondency, an ever-less-latent panic, as she made her way back from the bank where the same circumspect, taciturn woman had once again shaken her head and tersely informed her that no deposit had been made to her account, and Brulard had learned to despise this whole delightful setting, wondering in panic to what extent all these pretty things were laughing at her.

Had Jimmy not just raised that very question of money?

He'd started walking again, sharply tugging Brulard along, his pace brisker now, and Brulard thought he'd asked her an uncomfortable question about money. Brulard was feeling more carefree. She realized that, for her part (and it wasn't yet time to start suffering for Jimmy, and when that time did come her own good fortune would smother any overly burdensome remorse in Brulard, so she hoped), she had no real reason not to go on waiting and hoping. A delay, an unforeseen complication, something she didn't yet know of, something she would soon learn: that was probably the whole cause of her despair, because she didn't know. And, in a way, that ignorance wasn't real.

"Well?" Jimmy was asking in a troubled voice.

"Am I really here with you now?" Brulard asked in surprise.

"How are you managing financially?"

"Oh, I've got some money these last few days."

"From him? You sure?"

"Yes," Brulard firmly answered.

"Then. . ." (All at once Jimmy's voice was so slow, so quiet, that Brulard could scarcely hear it.) "If that's true, then I suppose. . . you might be able to help me out. It wouldn't have to be much, but. . ."

Brulard's thigh began to vibrate. With labored non-chalance, she took out her telephone. Uniformly tall, good-looking, and athletic, happy passers-by jostled her, not seeing her, with her diminutive build and, that morning, her gray face, and all around them, from what Brulard could make out here and there, the sole subject of conversation was the quality of the snow and the food.

The mountain had come closer. Now it was perfectly clear.

Brulard let out a small laugh, thinking: my mother never protected me from anything at all.

She held the telephone a few centimeters from her ear, saying nothing. Jimmy anxiously looked on, but she couldn't bring herself to give him a smile or still her trembling chin for his sake. Turning off her phone, she silenced the voice that was, beyond all doubt, speaking specifically to her, utter-ing her full name with such fury but also such hateful grief that her legs were still weak and burning hot.

Jimmy asked her no questions. Brulard concluded that he would ask her nothing more about these phone calls. He knows what all this is about, or can guess, from something he knows and I don't, something he knows I don't know, she thought, calmly perceptive, her mind suddenly clear, almost cold, impassive, capable of accepting the worst and not seek-ing it out but encouraging it, if it had to be, to reveal itself. What he knows and is afraid I might learn: that might even be why he came here, she went on to think. But is it because he wants me to know, or because he wants to make sure I don't?

"Jimmy, why did you come here?" said Brulard, very quietly, so as not to frighten him.

"To take you home with me. So you wouldn't be alone," said Jimmy, looking straight ahead, his jaw hardened.

A progressive reddening revealed a network of dilated capillaries on Jimmy's thin, hollow cheeks.

"What makes you think I'm alone?"

"I think you are. You're out walking with me and my dog, aren't you?"

And Brulard realized he was putting on this breezy display to conceal his discomfort and apprehension. Suddenly she saw him, despite his new clothes (new, but made of cheap leather, she observed), as a pitiful and ridiculous person, although often managing to hide it with a certain grace. Jimmy cut a sad figure, not that it was really his fault. Quickly and instinctively, she caressed his cheek. For had Jimmy ever once attained even a modicum of success in anything he'd done? Jimmy had made a life for himself, in a mediocre, half-baked way, always overestimating his abilities, and whenever luck smiled on him a little he wasted no time losing the money in cunning, vaguely demeaning ventures, such as, Brulard recalled, a certain kiosk built and manned by Jimmy in a suburban mall, where he offered to make his customers a pin bearing their likeness while they waited, with the aid of an implausible machine bought at an exorbitant price through a want ad, or else a pizzeria, sadly situated at the intersection of two highways, which Jimmy had taken over, aiming to make it a regular haunt for people in Brulard's circle, and which to this day he hadn't managed to sell, so strongly did the walls and the site exude failure, unhappiness, stupidity.

Now Jimmy was here, stubborn and tireless, hard-headedly confident in his ability to put up a good front, even if, as Brulard could see in the luminous air, the brilliant light of the lake, he'd so flagrantly and definitively aged—which is to say that no trick, no subtle arrangement of the hair on his forehead, or his high-buttoned shirts, could now prevent anyone noticing, before anything else, his hunched back, his bowed legs' irreversible thinness, the coarsened grain of his skin, the shadowy veil over his eyes, which, for a few seconds, when Jimmy thought himself out of sight, turned lost, evasive, and devious.

Exhausted, Brulard abruptly veered toward a bench on the edge of a vast lawn that sloped gently off to the lake. She sat down, despite the presence of Eve Brulard on the other end, the newly hostile and oppressive presence of a young Eve grown remarkably thin and bony. How this Eve Brulard looks like Lulu, Brulard said to herself, with a pang of displeasure and guilt. She pretended not to notice. She closed her eyes, fretfully wondering why the young Eve should now be appearing to her in the form of an enemy. When she half-opened her eyes, she noted that the splendid, high-spirited young people strolling past the bench were the very ones who'd jostled her in the streets of the old town.

"That's odd," she said cautiously.

Then Jimmy bent over and whispered in her ear:

"You see who's sitting over there?"

"Yes?"

"It's Lulu," said Jimmy with a stunned little scowl.

"Can that be?"

Brulard buried her face in her hands, shivering in fear and bewilderment. She thought she could hear Jimmy whispering, then nothing more, and when she peeked up again Jimmy had replaced the emaciated girl beside her. At her feet, the dog was looking up at her with what she could only interpret as avid affection. And those eternal young people from before strode by over and over, their long legs grazing Brulard's and Jimmy's knees. Did Jimmy realize that these abnormally healthy, good-looking young men and women seemed determined never to leave them again? Brulard wondered.

"What would Lulu be doing here?" she asked in an infuriated voice.

"I left her with the Alphonses. The plan was that the Alphonses would take her skiing," said Jimmy, casual and patient. "What, may I ask, is the problem with that? What is the problem?"

"Everywhere I hear people saying there's no more snow. So, you know, it's strange."

"There'll always be more than enough snow for fatsoes like the Alphonses and a kid like Lulu who can't stand snow," said Jimmy sententiously.

"But why should Lulu be so skinny all of a sudden?"

Jimmy kept quiet, in that heavy, mired way of his.

"So supposedly she got skinny, just like that, in the space

of a week?" said Brulard. "Because her mama chose to…"

She sniffed dubiously.

"I didn't notice what Lulu was wearing," she then said.

Jimmy's spirits revived, and he answered:

"She was wearing what I bought her for this Easter holiday with the Alphonses: a silver down coat with matching ski suit and fluorescent green ankle boots. I wanted her to make a good impression. The Alphonse girls have all that and much more."

"The girl I saw on the bench wasn't dressed in silver," said Brulard, calmly triumphant.

"No one who looks at you would ever say you're wearing loafers, because they couldn't imagine you wearing such shoes, and yet that's how it is, and you're wearing loafers," said Jimmy.

"Oh, why won't these young people leave us alone?" Brulard sighed, on the brink of tears.

They kept coming and going, three girls and two boys with similar builds, towering and long-limbed, their stiff, light blond hair down to the girls' shoulders, the boys' napes, and Brulard found in them a glacial, unearthly beauty that, far from delighting, pained the heart.

How worn, how faded seemed their two little selves, hers and Jimmy's, on their bench—how poor and ugly they were, crumpled under the wreckage of the life they'd led together, exasperated by each other exactly when they knew they'd be exasperated, knowing each other so well, so well, without tenderness or sympathy.

"Everything would be different if I had money, or even

just an inheritance to look forward to," said Jimmy with spiteful but placid assurance.

The memory of recent evenings when another man had spent freely for her pleasure, elegant dinners, outings to the opera and sophisticated bars, not with a view to seducing her, for she'd been long since seduced and in love, but simply to place that fine gem of love and seduction in a setting of conventional delights and established practices—those memories surfaced in Brulard's mind like episodes from a very ancient, irretrievable past, and while all that was desirable, delicious, it was also attached, now that Jimmy was here (poor, eternal Jimmy), to something vaguely and stupidly disloyal, even if she'd been drawn to the other man long before she knew how much he had.

But what could she do for Jimmy? What was she supposed to do for Jimmy, assuming she even could? And hadn't he in fact come here to do something for her, to come to her rescue, as much as to help himself? What gave him the idea (she'd seen his misgivings, his concern) that she needed to be rescued?

A violent migraine was battering the back of her skull. She couldn't speak a word. The young people began to laugh, howling in a way that struck Brulard as parodic and malevolent. Why were they so bent on following her, spying on her? Were they there beside her as friends? At the same time, if the idea was to keep watch over her, was such beauty uniformly distributed on five arrogant faces strictly necessary?

Could she see them as friends?

Brulard and Jimmy walked uphill toward the residential neighborhoods, toward the well-heeled heights overlooking the lake and the city, where Jimmy thought they would find the house he'd been told of. It was a chalet, brand new, made of blond wood, with deep eaves, multiple balconies laden with long chairs and poufs, cushions and dog toys: yellow hedgehogs, rubber bones, balls of all sorts.

Breathless from the climb, her skull painful and pounding, Brulard staggered and half-fell, one knee on the ground. Her shoe slipped off her foot. Jimmy was just bending down to pick up the loafer when a Great Dane burst out from behind the chalet, knocked Jimmy head over heels, and snatched up the shoe in its maw. It stood looking at them defiantly, with no intention of playing. Metallic glints gleamed in its short, gray fur. Jimmy's dog whined as it edged away, terrified, submissive. Not a sound from the chalet or anywhere around them, only the faint rustling of the larch trees, Jimmy's dog panting in fright.

Brulard stood up. She watched as Jimmy slowly crawled away, knees dragging over the gravel, and then, eyes fixed on the Great Dane, rose to his feet with calm, unhurried movements. She heard him whisper:

"Come on! Let's get out of here."

"What about my shoe?" said Brulard with a nervous little laugh.

She groaned and raised her hands to her head. The pain filled her eyes with stinging tears. Suddenly a man and woman appeared, and Brulard wasn't sure if they'd come from the house or the forest.

"The Rotors!" Jimmy murmured, with a delight that made it clear to Brulard just how afraid he had been.

Would the other man have felt such fear? Or were deluxe guard dogs his allies right from the start, by virtue of his upbringing? Brulard then wondered if Great Danes could smell the odor of money, of class, of chateaux, if they recognized the authority of elegant manners.

She closed her eyes for a brief moment. She heard Jimmy's insistent, beguiling voice, and from its slight desperate edge she realized he was playing his final card. Then Brulard heard the woman cordially exclaim:

"Why yes, of course, it's Jimmy Loire. Hello, Jimmy."

Brulard opened her eyes. Monsieur Rotor had disgustedly thrown the drool-soaked shoe at her feet.

"Come in, I'll lend you a pair of mine," said Madame Rotor, graciously.

Monsieur Rotor held back the Great Dane, his tanned face marked with the same severe and irascible expression as his dog's, and Jimmy took Brulard's arm to lead her toward the chalet. Brulard felt him shivering with relief, his terrified tension now waning. It wasn't the dog that had most frightened Jimmy. He was afraid of finding himself thrown off the property by a Rotor couple who had no memory of meeting him in Paris a few months before, at one of the many receptions Jimmy frequented, nervous and joyless, hoping to meet people in a position to give him work, Jimmy taking it as given that he could do anything so long as people explained what they expected. So, it flashed through Brulard's bored, morose mind, Jimmy must have enticed the Rotors efficiently enough to hear them toss out something like "Come by and visit us in the mountains." But, Brulard now wondered, attaching no great importance to the question, had she herself been an element in Jimmy's strategy from the start, or had the idea of bringing her along as a supporting player come to him only a little before, in the pizzeria where he'd insisted on taking her to dinner? Oh, what does it matter, Brulard had asked herself at the time, terrified by the prospect of any sort of resistance, what does one last bad pizza with Jimmy matter? Since after that everything will be over?

"They've seen the film. They'll recognize you, and I'll score big points," Jimmy had said, adorable, almost imploring.

Now, with a painful sense of vindication, Brulard observed that the middle-aged woman in her dark, out-of-place town clothes, trudging toward the Rotors' chalet with evident reluctance, half-dragged along by Jimmy Loire, her features clenched with migraine and exhaustion, quite clearly did not remind the Rotors of the yellow-scarved adventuress who played a minor but, according to Jimmy, indispensible and compelling role in *The Death of Claire Hassler.* Was that not exactly what he was whispering into Madame Rotor's ear? For she turned to cast Brulard a brief glance, surprised and polite, while Jimmy expressed his pride in his typical fashion, putting his hands on his thin hips and slightly puffing out his stomach, simultaneously displaying, Brulard was horrified to see, a pale green blot of olive-oil on his white shirt.

How was all this supposed to touch her now?

"I'd like... if you would, two or three aspirin."

The words hung before her lips as if someone else had whispered them beside her, in a comic falsetto.

"Eve Brulard..." Jimmy began.

"Is she feeling all right?"

"Just a little migraine... overwork..."

"Are you all right?"

"Eve Brulard, you know, who... Eve Brulard..."

"Is she all right?"

Brulard felt two firm hands pushing down on her shoulders, then the yielding surface of an armchair beneath her thighs. The chair dipped and rose.

At some point in the past, she was no longer sure when or in what, she used to play long scenes in a rocking chair, half-recumbent.

Could they stop rocking her? One more dip and she was going to bring up her pizza. Could they stop rocking her? How she was suffering—but what good would aspirin do? In spite of her spinning head, she sensed that she'd understood everything, though what she understood she didn't yet know, even as she knew it was only a matter of hours, perhaps minutes, before it all became clear. She understood, but, oh God, how she dreaded learning what it was that she understood.

Could they please stop rocking her, right now?

She spoke or kept silent, they heard her or didn't, impossible to say. A cold glass jarred her teeth, a bitter pill was dissolving on her tongue, too far back, next to her uvula. A dry hand stroked her cheek. She recognized Jimmy's hand, hot and anxious. Dear poor kind Jimmy, thought Brulard, nearly weeping with pity, had he understood, for his part, that it was all over? That she'd be lost to him forever as soon as they left the Rotors' chalet? He'd long been a deluded husband, but that was nothing next to the irreparable depreciation inflicted on his entire being, even his life story, his past, his name, since Brulard fell in love with another, so very much more glorious than Jimmy. But how to ensure that it all ended cleanly and definitively? Only, perhaps, Jimmy's instantaneous death, she couldn't help thinking, would deliver her of the disorder surrounding him, radiating expansively all around him, whereas the other one was all rigor, cool willfulness, precise desires.

"I thought... she was called Claire Hassler," said Madame Rotor, as if from a great distance, with a puzzled little laugh.

"Claire Hassler is only the name of the lead character, played by... oh, another actress."

That was Jimmy's voice, overly loud, at once incensed and incredulous, disgusted.

"Claire Hassler doesn't exist, for goodness' sake! It's a made-up name. It's a story."

"So who is Eva Brulard?" asked Madame Rotor, hesitantly.

"Eve Brulard. Not Eva. Eve. Eve Brulard. Eve Brulard."

"Who is she?"

"What my wife wants to know, I presume, is whether that's also the name of a character," pompously intervened a Monsieur Rotor who seemed to be standing just behind Brulard's back, as she thought she could feel his warm breath on her neck, odorless, thick, like a dog's.

So is that Rotor who's so hell-bent on rocking me? Brulard

wondered, exasperated. But was she really being rocked? Or was it the unraveling of all her senses that was giving her this continual up and down feeling?

She wished she could tell Jimmy to relax, that for her, and even more for him, it was in no way essential to convince the Rotors that she was a remarkable woman. But now Jimmy was losing his temper, she could tell by the sudden quickening of his words, although, for the Rotors who knew him so little, he might still have seemed simply the typical Parisian, sarcastic, belligerent, rude, and utterly unaware of it.

"You make me laugh," Jimmy was shouting. "Eve Brulard, a character? Don't tell me you of all people have never heard of Eve Brulard? So supposedly I live with a character?"

Jimmy, we don't live together anymore! Brulard exclaimed. We'll never live together again! Isn't that so? Relieved to find that the sound of her voice was not vibrating in her own ears, and that no one must have heard a word she had said, she shut her eyelids tight, determined to let herself be forgotten.

A doubt crept into Brulard's mind.

What proof did she have that she wasn't an impostor? For if she'd never acted in *The Death of Claire Hassler*, if the lovely woman in the yellow scarf was not Eve Brulard but some other actress, and if everywhere she went she nevertheless claimed, with Jimmy's complicity, that it was her, who would ever disabuse her?

She protested inwardly, indignant with herself for thinking such things. She did have a part in that movie. She remembered it with the most perfect clarity. Did she really remember? Nothing very precise at the moment, thanks to her crushing exhaustion, but she would, she would, as soon as she got some rest. Yes, would she remember? She thought it impossible to ask Jimmy for reassurance, not because this wasn't the time (Jimmy's mollified voice flowed like fresh, cool water all the way to the rocking chair, interspersed with Madame Rotor's appreciative "hmm!"s, and now the talk had apparently turned to some activity to be undertaken at once, a game to be organized before teatime, though of what sort Brulard had no idea), but because Brulard was now convinced that she'd have to be wary of Jimmy on that score as well.

On that score as well, she repeated to herself, tightly clutching the rocking chair's arms so as not to be sucked into the drain of the enormous avocado-green sink she could half see beneath her closed eyelids—identical to the one in the hotel bathroom, she noted with a knowing snicker, frightened and flattered to observe that once again it was all fitting together. If Jimmy was using her, if Jimmy was inventing roles and a career for her to fascinate the Rotors, how could she use him?

"Jimmy!" she called out, imperiously.

Now Brulard was looking out one of the chalet windows, toward the larches that rose almost to the roof. Monsieur Rotor and Jimmy were searching for something amid the stones and patches of snow, bending down, then cheerfully standing up again and heading into the blue shadows beneath the trees, while, from the edge of the woods, Madame Rotor urged them on with nods and grave little shouts, her hands in the pockets of her pale blue down coat, her long hair blowing free, graceful and golden.

These people are younger than we are, Brulard then told herself, with a pang in her heart.

Slowly she walked toward the front of the house and the opposite window, wearing the delicate red booties she'd been given, flat-heeled and a full size too small. Brulard thought she saw someone moving behind the Rotors' SUV. She pressed her forehead to the glass. She was just turning away, having seen nothing, when a brief vision of the two dogs, the Great Dane straddling Jimmy's mutt, brought her back to the window, alarmed. Jimmy's dog was invisible beneath the Great Dane's spine, which glistened as if coated with oil. Brulard saw her mangled shoe lying in front of the car.

She hurried away from the window and out the door to join Jimmy and the Rotors.

"You come look too," Madame Rotor called to her, jolly and affable.

Brulard trotted obediently toward the tall pines. A small smile of feigned triumph on his blue lips, Jimmy was displaying a chocolate rabbit with a pink ribbon.

"We put together several Easter-egg hunts like this every year," Monsieur Rotor was saying, visibly pleased with Jimmy. "What do you think, Loire?"

"It's great," said Jimmy. "I'm having a wonderful time."

"You're having a wonderful time?" asked Monsieur Rotor, at once gratified and vaguely dubious. "Looks to me like you're freezing, Loire."

"No," said Jimmy, "not at all."

"Well, your wife seems to be, Loire."

"Brulard. Eve Brulard," said Jimmy in a despairing voice.

Monsieur Rotor grunted, then suddenly bent over to pull a large nougat egg from beneath a small mound of moss.

Surely a bit later, but after a span of time that Brulard, mechanically digging through the snow and the pine needles, was unable to gauge (an hour or an afternoon or a full day), the frantic reappearance of Madame Rotor, who had gone in to make tea, broke the single-minded silence that reigned over the hunt.

"It's horrible," she cried. "Come see. No, not you, Jimmy, and you neither, Madame Loire. It's so horrible. Valentin's never done such a thing."

"Why, what did Valentin do?" Monsieur Rotor shot back, defensive.

"Your little dog, Jimmy...Valentin's torn him to pieces. That funny little dog of yours. He...ohh...he cut him in two!"

"I would never have expected that from Valentin," said Monsieur Rotor.

He looked at Jimmy, offended and disappointed.

"Valentin's so gentle," said Madame Rotor, hurt. "He's the most sensitive, loving animal I've ever known. Never had...a better dog than Valentin."

Brulard saw Jimmy's eyes darting miserably this way and that. He blushed violently, and Brulard was moved to observe that he had the face of an alcoholic. Lost, Jimmy stammered incomprehensibly.

"It's nothing," he finally mumbled. "Oh, it's nothing.

He…hadn't been my dog all that long."

He looked at Brulard with such anguish that she turned away, deeply pained, telling herself that from now on they were alone, apart, forever.

"You know what I'm craving? A nice fondue," Madame Rotor had said.

She'd draped her long blue down coat over her chair, and now she was sitting up very straight, her back nestled in the cushiony heart of her rich angelic raiment, glowing with such indisputable health, self-assurance, and youth that Brulard was half blinded, punch drunk.

They were sitting in a restaurant the Rotors had chosen. The Great Dane lay under the table, and Brulard saw the corners of Jimmy's dry lips twitch whenever Valentin licked his calf, which he did to Jimmy more than to anyone else.

Whisking her hair behind her neck with a silken toss of the head, Madame Rotor repeated in a very slightly authoritarian voice:

"Do you know what I'm craving?"

"A nice fondue," Jimmy murmured.

Lulu came in.

At first Brulard paid her only a distracted and weary sort of mind, for was this not yet another new form adopted by Eve Brulard in an attempt to convey all manner of unintelligible things? This Lulu, her short hair dyed orange (Brulard had left behind a Lulu with a long mane untouched since childhood), was entering in the wake of a loud, oversized family Brulard recognized as the Alphonses. Brulard had scrupulously avoided all contact with the Alphonses for years. She lowered her eyes. But how likely was it that Eve Brulard could divide herself into so many replicas, and take on the appearance of four expansive, guffawing Alphonses? It wasn't likely at all.

Lulu pulled out a chair and sat down with the same wondrous nonchalance as when she wore her hair long. Blinded and deafened by their own deafening racket, the Alphonses seemed not to have noticed Jimmy or Brulard. Then Lulu's eyes coldly met Brulard's, and Brulard realized that this was indeed her daughter Lulu, and not, by some miracle, herself as a girl.

Jimmy was very pale. He started to his feet, about to go talk to Lulu. Then he thought better of it and slowly turned away to hide from the Alphonses. Was he still thinking about his dog? Brulard wondered, deeply moved. Was he thinking about his dog with sadness and guilt?

Lulu was laughing with the Alphonses. The indecency of their laughter covered Brulard's forehead with a delicate cold sweat. She sensed Lulu's gaze, landing sometimes on her and sometimes on Jimmy, and that gaze, Brulard felt sure, was heavy with scorn and resentment. Were the four Alphonses, Lulu seemed to be saying, in their flawless camaraderie, in their full-hearted gaiety, not better than them, her inconstant, poisonous, penniless parents?

"Those people are very annoying," said Madame Rotor aloud.

She went on, her square chin extended toward Jimmy:

"Aren't those people annoying, incredibly annoying?

Loire?"

Surely alerted, thought Brulard, by the use of his last name rather than the usual jocose "Jimmy!," and also, thought Brulard, by the very perceptible cooling, which he must have felt just as she did, of his newfound relationship with the Rotors in the wake of the dog incident, which the Rotors unmistakably blamed on him, Jimmy thought it best to exclaim, in a sharp little voice:

"They are indeed! Very annoying."

Her parents were absolutely not to approach her, neither the one nor the other: that, Brulard realized, was what this young orange-haired Lulu was proclaiming, mutely but clearly, with her hard, vindictive gaze over the tables between them, protected by the beaming Alphonses, impregnable in their crassness. And also that her parents had betrayed her— and how was she supposed to get over that?

At the end of the meal, all through which Brulard felt only a vague awareness of her own silence, Madame Rotor picked up one of the many newspapers hung from wooden rods on the wall beside her. The wine had left her very merry and full of quips. As a joke, she read out the headlines, adopting a joyful tone when the news was grim, and a gloomy one when it was trivial. Brulard wasn't listening, and heard none of the words that involved her. Nevertheless, she saw Jimmy staring at her with a sort of panic.

"What an idea," said Monsieur Rotor, "doing yourself in when you've got it all. People in movies have it all. That guy had it all. Oh yes, they've got it all. Isn't that right, Loire?"

"I don't know anything about it," said Jimmy slowly,

never taking his eyes off Brulard.

The last tranquil, almost cold thought that came to Brulard was that no one had ever looked at her with so much compassion or friendship.

REVELATION

This woman and her son had walked the long road from their house to the bus stop, and because for two months it had rained without respite, not even one morning or a few hours in the night without rainfall, the road was now only a muddy trail between the plowed fields.

Now and then the son observed that you couldn't tell the road from the fields anymore, and the woman patiently pointed out that the fields were dark brown, almost black, apart from the glistening, stagnant puddles in the corners, while the waterlogged road was still a dull gray.

He nodded, as if thoroughly pleased with this answer. They walked on in silence for a few moments, then the son said again, as if making a startling discovery, "...can't tell the road from the fields, do you see," and within herself the woman was once again painfully surprised that he could repeat the most trivial thoughts with the same untarnished fascination, but she answered him gently, patient, detached, no longer listening to herself. And he nodded gravely, his brow clenched in concentration, and the woman's words seemed to her absurd and even enigmatic in their utter banality, and suddenly she wanted to laugh out loud at the both of them, at their senile prattle, but she did no such thing, she didn't even smile, knowing the son was now beyond all understanding or perception of irony. That thought left her morose until her son said again: "...isn't it funny, you can't tell the...," turning toward her in search of an explanation, then her irritation and torment banished all sadness for a time, and the woman carefully put on a voice and expression adapted to what she thought she knew of the thing in him that was broken, the thing that had broken.

He's unbearable, she sometimes thought. And also: he seems not so much insane as stupid, appallingly stupid.

She was angry with herself for that. This son was not cruel. His capacity for meanness had waned even as the mother's aggressive rancor grew. She realized that her despair and her rage were fueled by nothing other than the progressive disappearance of those emotions in the son.

No, this son wasn't cruel, alas. And they would both take the bus to Rouen, since the rain had at long last stopped falling, but that evening the woman would come home to Corneville alone.

She'd take the bus back in the other direction, and the son wouldn't be with her, and maybe he knew that and maybe he didn't, it was too late now to find out. He might then abruptly refuse to get onto the bus, and the woman pictured him standing still by the roadside, calmly shaking his head and repeating, calm and incredulous: what an idea, mama, what an idea.

They were reaching the end of the road, and now they were nearing the sign that marked the stop, on the grassy strip between the fields and the highway. The sign was leaning and rusted. On it she could read the name *Corneville*. Could her son still do the same? She wanted to spit out at him, in her hard voice: So what do you think? You think you're going to come home with me tonight? You think you'll be coming home someday?

The sky suddenly cleared, and at the same instant the bus braked in front of them—appearing, the woman thought, in a flood of sunlight that nothing could have foretold. So long ago had all radiance disappeared from the atmosphere that the woman's eyes stung. She squinted, scowled. Close at her side, the son raised his head and smiled broadly. "Mama," he murmured, "oh, mama, isn't it peculiar!" And, as always when he opened his mouth, she found herself irritated beyond all reason. She had to restrain herself from snapping back at him: You think there's anything on this earth as peculiar as you? Instead, she pushed him indelicately toward the bus door, which had just opened with a sort of deep, weary sigh.

This son never showed any unhappiness at being treated little better than the dog of the house, and the woman was not unaware that she often took advantage of that, raising her voice to him, shoving him aside needlessly, but pained to see him so unaffected by these small humiliations, by his own lack of dignity, and then trying in vain, knowing perfectly well it was pointless, to rouse him to even the most fleeting fit of anger.

Nevertheless, she whispered when she asked the driver

for one round-trip ticket and one one-way.

Yes, she wanted him to resist, she thought bitterly, but not about this.

The son was starting toward the narrow aisle between the two rows of seats when the driver caught sight of him. He stopped looking at the woman and stared at the son's face, then at his back, his pale little eyes suddenly filling with wonder and, she observed, mystified, with unconcealed, cordial admiration. And when the son sat down toward the middle of the bus, on the aisle so he could stretch out his long legs, the driver went on gazing at him in the rear-view mirror with a wise smile on his lips.

The driver was not a young man.

Clutching her money, the woman waited for the thought of handing over the tickets to occur to him. He shook his head, as if trying to wake himself. Finally he turned toward her, his gaze still veiled by an airy, distracted pleasure.

As time went by and the bus rolled down the road through the fields in this sudden abundance of light, the woman noticed the other passengers often turning around toward the son, or eyeing him furtively, she saw their benevolence and delight, and she realized that the son, this endlessly troublesome son, noticed none of it. She felt her own face grow pink with guilt and incomprehension. She hid it by looking out the window. She told herself she was in this bus as if in the heart of a country so utterly foreign that every gesture of those around her was beyond her understanding. Every face was nevertheless of a type she knew well: wizened old ladies in beige raincoats, a farmer in glasses with smoked lenses, teenagers on their way home from school, a woman who resembled her in every way.

But why were they all staring at her son?

And why did the simple act of turning their gaze toward that son's beatific, distant face seem to illuminate them with such happiness?

She couldn't understand. None of them realized: there was no way to live with a son such as hers, and yet she thought this so utterly self-evident that people would do anything to avoid laying eyes on him.

The heat and the rumble of the bus left her drowsy. As long as the journey went on, there were no decisions of any kind to be made. She could scarcely bring herself to imagine the moment when she'd have to get off the bus and turn her thoughts to her son, and begin silently plotting.

Was this son, she suddenly thought, some animal she was going to sell at the market in Rouen? Was she ridding herself of him for personal gain? No, no—she smiled wearily—it was simply intolerable, infuriating, to have him beside you, under your roof, breathing the same air as you, this son with his mysterious manias, his stifling, monotonous thoughts.

When the bus stopped at Saint-Wandrille, the woman half rose from her seat to glance at the broad rear-view mirror. She saw exactly what she was expecting—the two pale slits of the driver's eyes fixed on her son, on the reflection of his face over the seatbacks, the son's handsome, calm face, she thought to herself in amazement, and she wondered, incredulous, sardonic, if the driver and all the others openly staring at the son's face realized that that face was so beautiful and so calm only because it had no awareness of the loving attention it inspired, and so beautiful and so calm that the time had now come to put it away, never again to be seen in the streets of Corneville, and, at home, never again to burden the atmosphere with its oppressive, unending presence.

This woman thought that she couldn't bear the beauty of that son's face one moment longer—and that, in the old days, when he was still right, his face was never as handsome. No one would have turned to look at the son back when there was no need to keep from him where he was being taken. His face then had no reason to be as beautiful as it was now, since it expressed only ordinary thoughts. Nevertheless, thought the woman, rebelling, no one had the right to demand that she feel grateful or pleased at this change, no one could ask her to admire that face herself, however handsome and calm it may be.

She whispered in his ear: "I'll be coming back to Corneville without you."

"I know," he said.

He smiled at her, amiable, reassuring. He went so far as to pat her arm, and then she couldn't help confiding that she wished the bus would never stop, which the son, he told her, understood perfectly. Those other sons of hers wouldn't have understood at all, it occurred to her, and she missed this one already. She'd be coming home alone, thank God: how she would miss him!